The Me and Elsie Chronicles (and Jen too)

by
M. L. Buchman

Solar Stupid originally published 2013

Moon Shine originally appeared in *Fiction River: Moonscapes* (2014)

Cover images:
Woman Astronaut We Can Do It The Power
Of Protest © Studiostoks | Dreamstime.com

Buchman Bookworks

Other works by M.L. Buchman

<u>The Night Stalkers</u>

MAIN FLIGHT
The Night Is Mine
I Own the Dawn
Wait Until Dark
Take Over at Midnight
Light Up the Night
Bring On the Dusk
By Break of Day

WHITE HOUSE HOLIDAY
Daniel's Christmas
Frank's Independence Day
Peter's Christmas
Zachary's Christmas
Roy's Independence Day

AND THE NAVY
Christmas at Steel Beach
Christmas at Peleliu Cove

5E
Target of the Heart
Target Lock on Love

<u>Firehawks</u>

MAIN FLIGHT
Pure Heat
Full Blaze
Hot Point
Flash of Fire

Welcome to My Stories

Here's some stories I writ down. Done it 'cause my best friend Jen said I oughta—what with us being some of the first gals to haul cargo 'cross the black reaches of the Up'n'up and all. She said I should put in some of the wisdom I learnt from Pap too 'cause he raised me up so fine. I always do what she says what with her being so smart and all.

So here's some of how I got my first ship *Elsie.* There's some of how me and Jen was flyin' for Planetary Engineering, workin' them space lanes, and other bits 'bout the wonderful kinda men we met up with while stopping off at

Tycho Tavern, Low-Gee Lounge on Mars, and the Europa LaunchPub (one a my personal-type favorites).

Intro to: Launch Party

Some people been asking if I writ all these stories in order and I gotta tell you I didn't. I just writ 'em down as they come to me. See, I come from a whole long line of storyteller types and it's more 'bout telling the right story, not so much of when it happened.

It always makes me wonder that Jen says she wasn't much at telling stories.

"What did you do to evenings?" I'd ask her.

"Clubbing," she shrugged. "Movies, fancy dinners, whatever. What about you?"

Well, me and Pap, and maybe two or three of the other locals, was likely to be sitting around Pap's still on quiet evenings. Cooking a mash ain't smokeless, even if you use good hickory and oak for the fire. That meant most times we'd cook at night so as the revenooer men didn't bother us none.

Now once a mash is running, ain't so much to do except feeding a log now and then and maybe watching the stars some. So we'd sit around jawing or telling a story or two. Maybe doin' some other things once I got old enough to take an interest in all that. So I guess I just come by my storytelling natural-like.

I think that's where I fell in love with them stars too. On quiet nights with nothing but the bats and a screech owl goin' by, it was like you could reach out and touch them points of light.

Pap liked that I knew the stars so good. I could use 'em to help him navigate at night when we wanted to move a shipment real quiet-like. Got to the point where I could read the time easy as a clock just by lookin' aloft and knowin' the date.

"You didn't have nothing like that growing up?" I asked Jen again.

"There's always a good party somewhere.

Plenty to drink and plenty of men." Jen had the right kinda shape to get menfolk to pay close attention and the pretty blond hair to go with it.

Me, I always feel like I gotta duck going through a door. I'm not big around, well, except in certain places menfolk seem to like, but I'm a big gal. 'Sides, I'm more the quiet-type and Jen is got this big smile and laugh that can make the whole world brighter. Exceptin' when I ask her 'bout her past. Then she gets all sad and even quieter'n me, so I try not to ask much.

I wrote this story for Jen 'cause I think she should see what kinda party I grew up havin'.

LAUNCH PARTY

*"**Now you be smart** up there, girl. The Up'n'up ain't no place to be foolin' about none."*

My pap always gave good advice so I was doin' my best to listen close. It was a might difficult 'cause he was giving me a real nice going away party. Pap was so sweet, I was gonna miss him something awful when I got into space tomorrow. I wrapped him into a big hug.

He reached as far around my big shoulders as he could and gave me a friendly pat on the back. Pap weren't a big man. Wasn't much for showin' just anyone how he felt neither, but I was his only kin other than an uncle neither of us ever mentioned and a brother that was still doing time for being stupid. Pap had no patience for stupid.

"I'll be smart, Pap. Promise." I raised my mason jar still half-full of Pap's very best moonshine and he done the same. We toasted and we drank.

Might not be much kin around, seeing as I was his only sprout worth mentioning and hadn't done nothing myself about making more of them, but it was a cheery crowd. A lot of the locals came by.

Even Tom had come out to our old cabin and left his sheriff's badge at home. His deputy wasn't quite as sharp, but had tucked his own badge away quick enough that nobody held it against him none. The neighbor gals had come by and was teasing him something fierce because he was a handsome man even if he worked for Johnny Law. He had an extra-good quality in the gals' eyes because he weren't married to nobody yet neither.

My money was on Nancy, but Betsy was a long way from folding her cards just yet. Then Jake strolled in and I had a few thoughts myself on what kinda send-off I was gonna be getting. Jake and I had more than a few tussles in the hay and his smile said he was thinking about them times too. He'd always been a good sort. Seeing me and Pap having a jaw, he just shook Pap's hand, winked at me some, poured himself a jar of hootch, and went to join in the fun of teasing Johnny Law.

Pap probably would have taken him on as an assistant, if Jake weren't so interested in cattle (he liked to pick up strays, real quiet-like, from all sorts of strange places, and sell 'em just as quiet in other places). I could cook 'shine 'most as good as Pap, but my heart wasn't in the business side. There's a whole lot more to moonshine than just running a still.

Wasn't long afore Sue was in Jake's lap, but the way he kept looking over to me, I saw he was just passing the time and I weren't much of a jealous sort anyhow.

"Thing's is different up there," Pap was talking. He was so wise that he still made sense right up to the moment he falls over from too much liquor—and he has a prodigious capacity from so much practice, more than any man nor woman I ever laid eyes on. He was a long way from falling over yet, so I set into listening. "Cain't just dodge and weave and go down a dirt road with your lights off in a big old ship."

I'd tried to explain how huge a Class Four cargo hauler was, but it was a tricky thing to do. Telling him she was a couple times bigger than a Boeing jet didn't help much as he'd never been on a plane. I wasn't sure he'd ever been out of the county except when dodging from swamp up into the hills to get away from Tom or his deputy who now had Nancy on one knee, Betsy on the other, and didn't know which dress he was supposed to be looking down the front of.

Being a gal bigger than Nancy, Betsy, and Sue all bundled together made me feel just that much closer to the ship I was getting tomorrow. Well, maybe not Betsy, she's a hefty gal herself, but more round the middle than me. Betsy was big enough around that she was always about to fall out of her dresses. Of course the boys didn't mind as she did such a fine job of landing on her back whenever it happened.

I'm just big-framed.

"You was born king-sized and wouldn't listen to nobody about when to stop growing," Pap often said. I could hear the secret kinda pride he had in me.

Pap did kinda catch on how big my ship was when I told him that I could carry all the 'shine he'd ever cooked in a single run and still have room left over for all the 'shine he ever wanted to cook. Pap finally understood that, as he was a man with a big imagination when it come to his 'shine.

"You keep your eye on what's important," he said and I could see that Pap was done. I hugged him again just 'cause I was gonna miss him and his advising so.

After some more drinking and eating, Jake had brought a fatted calf—though he wasn't sayin' whose and we wasn't asking—and we roasted it up real nice over a big fire.

Jake's send-off that night was as fine as a gal could ask for. We came darn near to igniting the hay up in that loft we went at it so.

I was feeling all loose-hipped and only a little loose-headed when I was fixin' to go the next morning. I'd told Pap he'd be okay on the bus, nobody checked papers on a bus to see if you had outstanding warrants in a couple a states, but he just shook his head. With Jake still snoozing in the hayloft and the deputy still snoring between Nancy and Sue—wasn't sure just who Betsy had finally gone off with—I left real quiet. Pap drove me down to the station and I could see how it hurt him to let me go, so neither of us even waved as he drove off.

The bit a sleep on the train perked me up some and I rolled into Canaveral ready to go. I'd done all my trainin' and flown my check rides. My ship was just waitin' for me up in orbit. She could land on any of the hard planets 'cepting Earth. And there weren't nothing to land on at the gas planets, just a whole lot of atmo that could crush you even flatter than smacking into a hard planet without slowing down some first. So I was just cargo on my way to the Up'n'up.

I'd already been through the pre-launch briefings a couple of times. I mean I could give the pre-launch briefing in my sleep, so that's just what I did, catchin' me a few more winks afore we hit zero-gee.

I gotta admit, that was one of the things that attracted me to flying ships above the sky. I knew I still had mass and all, but things weren't always dragging toward the ground so much. I got a bra bigger'n those stick-girl models' entire dresses in them magazines. Zero-gee, don't need no such extra help holding things up, which the menfolk really seemed to appreciate.

But there was one surprise I wasn't ready for when I reached my ship.

"She's new," the Planetary Engineering representative said while admirin' exactly the sort of thing I was just talking about.

He wasn't built like Jake, but he weren't a scrawny little wizard like Pap neither. I might have paid him some more attention if it weren't for the next thing he said.

"She needs a name. You get to pick it out."

I hadn't thought none 'bout getting to name my ship. I thunk on it a bit, wishing I had a beer to lubricate my thinking. I had a case of Pap's 'shine that he'd given me as a going away present, but I wasn't gonna share that with no PE rep, not even if he had been as good looking as Jake was—who was a handsome devil and knew it.

Instead, I stared out the viewport and

watched my ship. A Class Four weren't exactly graceful, but she was designed to land in thin atmo like on Mars, Venus, and them sorts of places. She sure weren't as ungainly as the deep-space craft that was never gonna land nowhere.

Looking at her, she kinda reminded me of Ma. Pap had never been much of one for cameras and such, but he'd told me about her plenty over the years. Least once or twice.

"Good gal, your ma. Too bad she ran off with that trucker, she'd a liked you once you were growed. You weren't nothing but a pain in the ass 'til then," but he said it with love and affection because he had so much of that in him.

Pap didn't blame her none for leaving.

"Your ma always had big dreams, just like you. That's the kinda gal she was. Guess she had to go off to find 'em."

Well, it was Ma's example what led me to space. We was just a big dreaming type of family.

"Her name is *Elsie*," I told the PE rep. And while the crew was out painting her name on the outside, that rep kinda helped me christen her on the inside. I did break out a bottle of Pap's 'shine to share and we had a good old time doing the sharing and christening and all.

Finally had to shoo him off otherwise I'd never get me around to breaking orbit. See, there ain't a whole lot of gals working the skyways. It was another piece of what got me interested in space.

This recruiter who come by our school yammered on and on about opportunity and the growing need for skilled labor in the conquest of space. He weren't much good at it though, he'd never get no passing grade from Mrs. Clement in speech class with how bored he looked. But I perked right up when he mentioned the money, as good in a year as Pap had probably made in ten even as the best 'shiner in the state.

Then that recruiter man talked about there bein' one women for every ten men and I signed up right off! Them was my kinda odds. Couldn't get the others to see it my way, not even Sue who I always thought was the smartest of all us gals. I figure it was 'cause they didn't have the big picture learnin' that Pap had given me.

Well, I'd listened and here I was. Just rarin' to go.

Now, for a gal to break orbit in her own ship named for her ma was pretty special. The Planetary Engineering representative told me my first load was a-waitin' for me up at Tycho Base on old Luna. Then he slipped off-ship with the tail end of Pap's bottle, but I had me the rest of a case yet. Hadn't wanted to use it so much, but as I said, this was a special occasion.

I opened a second bottle and fired off *Elsie's* engine. Together we lit up the sky, what with me breaking out my fine singing voice and all.

Now there's this trick in space.

On a lake, your engine stops working and you slow down real quick. Even a car works like that. Run outta fuel when you're trying to get off and away somewhere real snappy, you come to a stop awful sudden-like.

That's why you gotta make sure the tank is always full before startin' on a important delivery. As I said, moonshining ain't just about running a still. A girl's gotta know things.

Like driving in space is total different from drivin' a boat or a car on a dark gravel road. Space is more like driving over a big ol' mountain. You heave and ho and huff and puff 'til you climb up high out of that old gravity well. Then slow at first, but always gaining speed, you ride up over that gravity crest. Suddenly the Earth ain't holding you back none and the moon is pulling you in faster and faster.

Now some folks say you tap on the brakes the whole way down. Others say you let her roll, take the wild ride, and then brake at the end. Running 'shine I'd learned long ago that you take that wild ride, sometimes even shuttin' the motor off too so you're moving real quiet-like.

I was having this and some other deep thoughts, like imagining my first trip to the Tycho Tavern and Grill and my first taste of moon beer and such, as I came down toward Tycho.

First thing I noticed after a little nap was old Luna had grown a might larger than when I left Earth. Second thing was there was a whole bunch of lights lit up bright as a Christmas tree on my comm panel. More was lightin' up every moment.

Figured I should most probably check out

this Luna-growing thing first, what with her getting bigger by the second.

Turned out I was way closer than I thought. Luna is a whole lot smaller than Earth and that did funny things to the curve of the horizon making you think she was farther away. I supposed that I could peel off, take an extra orbit on my way in, though even that was looking to be tricky.

So, I went for the old 'shiner's option. I flipped *Elsie* so she was tail down and let loose with a blast big enough to clear a Moose Lodge during a Friday social. It was hard burn all the ways down, exhaust going every which way. Now them red lights on my comm panel lit up even brighter until I pulled the circuit breaker on that stuff—too busy to be doing any blathering anyway.

I got the Elsie down on her tush as sweet as one a them English queens on her royal backside. 'Course the landing gantry had a kinda odd tilt to it. Maybe they built 'em different on the moon because of the gravity difference, all melted-like.

Now if you're gonna celebrate something, like say your first trip to the moon, there ain't no better place to go on Luna but the Tycho Tavern and Grill. Mighta forgot to turn my comms back on in my hurry, but soon as I saw the place, I figured I'd check on that later.

Tycho is the first-ever settlement in the Up'n'up. Pap could remember when it wasn't even there, but Pap was older than the hills so that shouldn't surprise none. It was down in a tunnel. One of them science boys had found the big ol' iron-nickel meteor what had punched the big hole in Luna's side—musta really been something to see—and they'd mined it out. Of course miners are almost as smart as us space pilots. The first thing they done was put a pub in the big old hole where the meteor had been.

They lit it all dim and mysterious-like, though my eyes adapted soon enough after staring at the my bright old landing burn splashing up against the ground so hard. A girl who runs 'shine when her Pap is sleeping through a delivery—knackered from working as hard as he does—has to have eyes that adapt right quick.

Just like promised, the place was packed thick with menfolk.

"You're new!" A woman took hold of my elbow and was staring up at me. We was about as different as could be. She was shoulder-high, with soft flowy blond hair instead of my scraggle mop. She was all trim except for the kinda curves I knew menfolk were especial partial to. She had plenty of those.

"I'm Jen. Come on! Sit with me!" And she was draggin' me off sideways before I had me a chance to survey the menfolk proper. "I've got a fresh pitcher of beer."

Well, she didn't have to ask me twice.

"You're only the third one, you know. Female pilot in the Up'n'up. And Evgenia's a total bitch. Of course, wouldn't you be if you had a name like that? Grew up in Moscow or South Africa or one of those foreign places. I was from Hawaii. I hit the Up'n'up before the volcano blew and wiped it all out. Are you a bitch?"

When I done told her I was a human-type person, not a dog-type person, she laughed big as a house and smacked me good on the shoulder.

"Oh, we're going to be best friends. I can just tell."

Not sure if I ever had me a best friend before, so I agreed and suddenly we was. I suppose that was just the way that things happened around Jen.

Next thing I knowed we was picking out men. "No, not Vaco. He kisses worse than a tenth-grade rich boy."

Never met no rich boy, but I caught her meaning.

"And old Jackie is a crazy sum-bitch, but not in a good-way crazy, if you know what I mean."

I didn't, but if you don't trust your best friend, you don't trust nobody.

"Hey, Jen." A pair of likely specimens came walking up to the table. They was very nice-looking to my eye. All spiffy in fancy uniforms.

"Hey yourself, Cash. Ty."

Then I noticed something odd going on behind them. Like the bar was fading. People was leavin' all quiet-like and they was doing it quick. Downright tip-toeing along at one-sixth gravity, which looked kinda funny with how they was bouncing up and down. Can't say as I noticed the low gravity much myself except maybe the way it wasn't dragging on my big old melons so hard, but we pilots got weightless training afore we was hired.

Then I looked back at the uniforms a bit more and I begun to guess why everyone was scootin'. It weren't no Earth uniform, least not that we see in the hill country back to home. But it was like when Tom and his deputy got all dressed up for the Fourth of July parade.

They was Johnny Law.

My new best friend Jen stayed solid as a rock, so I stayed with her. 'Sides, I'd just been settin' here drinking my first Luna beer, so couldn't imagine they might be wantin' to jaw with me none.

But they did, both turnin' to look to me.

"You the one who came down so hot and heavy on Pad Four?"

I was pretty pleased with that landing and told 'em so.

"You melted the gantry!"

"Now, Cash," Jen cut him off. "It isn't nice to be shouting at the newest woman pilot, especially after her very first landing." Somehow her shirt had opened a button or two while no one was watching, enough that

I could see Jen's curves was all Jen and no padding.

"But—"

"Ty," Jen stopped him as smooth as could be. "I think we can find a way to make this all okay."

"Oh, and how's that?"

But Jen wasn't lookin' at them, she was lookin' at me. She raised an eyebrow at me in a kinda question sorta way. Had a smile on fit to beat the band too.

Now I thought me back to another piece of Pap's good advice.

"Always good to know the right sorta people, girl. They can help you in all sorts of ways." He told me that right after Tom had caught up with Pap one night—a hard thing to do as Pap was as slippery as they come in the 'shining business—and Pap had rewarded him with a full jug of his latest brew.

So I looked back at Jen. If your best friend ain't the right sorta people then wasn't no one who was. I couldn't do that one-eyebrow kinda thing, but I could wink just fine—so I sent Jen a big old one.

We kinda scooted together, makin' just

enough room for the two men in their pretty uniforms to join us at the table. I might of slipped a button or two on my own shirt real subtle-like whilst I was doin' the moving.

Now Jake had given me a fine send-off at Pap's going-away party.

Looked like these boys were ready to give me a big old welcome. Exactly the kinda launch party this gal could learn to appreciate.

Intro to: Solar Stupid

This here is the first story I writ down. This writing come about 'cause when I done told Jen this story she was laughin' so hard I thought she was chokin'.

"No, it's true. It's so true. Solar stupid! I *love* it!"

Now when your best friend gets that excited it just ain't polite to not go along for the ride.

I kinda had this voice in my head. Just rang in clear as a bell when I was tellin' 'bout my adventures down the way toward Mama Sol. First thing we did, well, after a couple of men helped us take care of a few other things, was to gather round the folk at the LaunchPub—out on Europa, don't ya know.

"Tell them," Jen prompted me.

Well there was just us two gals and a dozen other space driver types. Then there was another dozen locals and a bartender type. I'd never tried to speak to no crowd so large and I started into hemmin' and hawin' tryin' to figure out how to tell the story proper.

"No!" Jen stopped me. "Just tell it like you told it to me."

I looked out at the waiting folk. See, not many gals makin' the jump out of Earth atmo to fly the Up'n'up, you know, so we tend to draw somethin' of a crowd just by breathin'.

"Here," Jen shifted so she was sittin' across from me. "Just tell it to me."

Ralphie slipped into the seat close beside me, taking some advantage of Jen movin' aside. I'd heard some about Ralphie, that I tell later on, so I was lookin' forward something fierce to what else was gonna happen that night after the storytelling and the drinking and all.

Then I thought of something Pap would say when I was bein' all shy about something:

"Go on, girl. Speak your piece and get 'er done."

Like I said before, Pap always gave the best advice.

So, here's that story, way I told it in the LaunchPub on Europa that night. And no, I won't be tellin' the story on Ralphie 'cause that ain't somethin' a girl does if she were raised proper. You want good Ralphie stories, y'all better ask Jen. She's better'n me at telling that type of story anyways. If she do tell though, listen close, 'cause it'll be a good one.

SOLAR STUPID

I'd prowled through some seedy dives before. Of course that was all there seemed to be in the Up'n'up. Once a gal cracked Earth's atmo, well, it wasn't like sittin' around Pap's still under the moonlight and sipping a jar of corn 'shine while it's still warm from drippin' off the condenser.

I'd been around some since I first launched. Picked up men out on Titan while looking at Saturn's big old rings whirling about the sky. I certainly managed to drag down more than my fair share of able male bodies at Tycho City, 'course being one of the few gal types trucking across the big black emptiness, I was kinda in short supply and I admit that I like that some.

The best spot I ever found was in the dark recesses of Europa's LaunchPub, suckin' down brews made from the ocean that washed a hundred meters below the surface ice and then humpin' some man blind.

But Mercury station, that sure were something else.

First, one look at the planet was enough to make a lady sling her rig down through the old gravity well and just move her load right on back up-system. What idiot back in Planetary Engineering decided that this half-frozen, half-baked planet needed a terraforming anyway? It was like them folks at PE was just lookin' for ways to 'cause trouble. And when they caused theyselves that kinda thing, well, it just came on down the old disposal pipe to land on folks like me and Jen.

Worse yet, they had me land two thousand klicks from the one lousy base to set down my load. They was sittin' pretty as could be at the north pole, and I was all the way down on the equator. How's a girl supposed to get a decent drink and an overeager man when Mercury base is a whole three-day rolligon journey 'cross the mess these people call a terrain? It's worse than the swamps back home…only not so wet.

They had me land on the dark side, which I guess was okay. It was all icy and would be for another Mercury year. The planet only made one extra turn for every two trips around Mama Sol. So one side is a coupla times the melting point of lead, and t'other side is way below the freezing point of pure alcohol— even Pap's purest don't stand a chance there.

I had to use lights to see anything, but the stars were sure pretty and the sun wasn't trying to cook my brain like it would on the daylight side, so that part was okay.

Maybe I was just feeling down a bit. I was usual a pretty cheery sort. My best friend Jen was always telling me I was, and someone as cheery as Jen says something like that, well, I sure believed her.

Just six weeks ago she and I had been constructing an L2 Habitat off the backside of old Luna. We'd been havin' a grand time hauling chunks of Plas up out of Luna's gravity well, gettin' a man and gettin' down at the Tycho Tavern in between runs. Got to use me a fabricating torch a bit, too, which wasn't all that hard. Pap's still always needed patchin' of one sort or another and Pap finally told me one day that I was a better hand at fabricatin' than anybody he'd ever seed.

Touched me right in the old heart it did. Pap was always saying the sweetest things to me, encouraging me when I was just a little tyke. Not that that lasted so long, what with me growing up to be such a big gal and all, but them was good memories.

Problem was, having proved I knew which end of a torch wasn't going to melt my suit if'n I held onto it too long, PE changed the kinda jobs they was givin' me.

Now, Jen, she didn't have that kinda touch. She grew up in some fancy city what didn't exist no more. She knew all kinds a things about men and getting her way, but not the sort a things like how to patch a still after some revenooer man shot it all up and left it for dead.

They pulled me off the L2 Habitat job and sent me on down the gravity well. I was just glad they was paying the fuel bill, as it was gonna be a long climb back up to Earth once this here job was done.

So, after six weeks of dry space going down, I start unloading the gear without a proper kind of break.

I let 'em know at Mercury Base I was working on their project and could use a friendly old hand—especial if it were attached to a big handsome man.

Not a peep outta them people!

Now, mining-bots can be a great help, once you have them set up. On my own, that was a week right there.

They never worked the way they shoulda comin' out of the box. Always had all their settings wrong, no imagination in them PE people. I spent an extra couple days tinkering with them until they could really do some things without me having to tell them every little step. You open up their heads, rearrange some memory chips on the B4 decision buss, and they can take on a whole week of tasks in one gulp. Gets messy when they miss a step or two, but I figure none of this is like rocket science. After all, I fly a rocket, so I kinda figure I know better than some PE gal sittin' back on Earth.

Once that was all done, then we—me and the bots, 'cause there still weren't no menfolk about—unloaded the mass drivers and started drilling the anchor holes.

That whiz-gal back at Planetary Engineering—what with her degrees and all but who'd clearly never crossed atmo into the Up'n'up—musta cooked up this stupid idea while scratching herself and wondering what she'd feed her cat for dinner.

Me and Pap was practical, we knew cats fed theyselves jes' fine on mice and all. But Jen tells me that city folk got some strange ideas 'bout that.

So she musta been right busy scratching herself instead of having some nice man doin' it for her when she wrote out: "Set up a rack of mass drivers along the equator of Mercury." That's what had come out of her big science brain and so that's what I was doing.

Once them drivers was anchored, with a couple hundred mining-bots to feed them, I'd fire them off—all pointing in the same direction. Bots would feed bits of Mercury, rocks and ice and like that, into the hoppers and the mass drivers fire like mad for twenty years or so and then…the whole stupid thing starts to spin faster'n once every two years.

Then, instead of having a planet with one side the temperature of deep space and the other side way the heck above the lead melting point, you get a spinning boulder that no one cares about an' that's still too darned toasty all over to fry an egg. It would just hit the surface and flash into steam before it could cook.

Now my Pap would have a thing or two to say about this. It would be something wise, 'cause that's the way Pap is. Something like:

"Don't be messing with Mother Nature. She got her mind set in her ways, so you best let her be. And always watch the pressure gauge close." He'd said that while watchin' a fishing pole that no fish had showed no interest in biting on. Not in so long that he'd worked his way through a whole jug of his best 'shine while waitin'. He didn't mind, he was that kinda fisherman, my Pap.

Or maybe:

"Them people got no more common sense than my damn pig."

Pap had an amazing way with words.

But you try to point all this out to them engineers and they tell you you're just a dumb rocket jock and ain't smart like they is.

They're all whacked on Earth.

Up-system they ain't nearly as bizarre. By the time you haul your sorry behind across the asteroid belt, everything gets lots mellower and much less stupid.

Maybe stupidness compresses more and more as you get down toward the sun. Solar stupid could explain a whole lot of things.

Like some other PE gal's—or maybe it were the same one—fine plan to break Venus' cloud layer and let the sun shine in by ionizing the atmosphere to turn it all into rain. First off, any moisture that would land on that surface would just flash back into steam and make new clouds right away anyways. Second, nobody figured out ahead a time that settin' off the thirty nucs simultaneously might react funny with the atmosphere and irradiate the planet for the next couple dozen half-lives of Thorium 229. They could try again in another seventy-thousand years or so. If they was feeling brave.

Now instead of just being a hot, dead planet under a bank of clouds, it's a hot, dead, radioactive planet under a bank of clouds.

Solar stupid.

Couldn't wait to see Jen and tell her about that idea.

"That's it," she'd say and let loose one of her big crows of delight. I missed Jen. She was always after something to laugh about.

Weren't a thing here on Mercury's dark side to make a girl giggle.

So after three weeks of me and the bots setting up them drivers in the cold and dark of the space-side, and me moving the ship three times to place the drivers, with no help from the lazy dogs at Mercury base, it was all good to go. Then I lifted a few hundred klicks up in case one of them blew or something else nasty…maybe I shouldn'ta had them mining bots do so much of the assembling too. I didn't want to be marooned too far from the nearest beer if we got a planet quake or somethin'.

I decided to jes' sit back and let them ground-pounders have a rough ride. Pap had taught me about that good:

"There's the folks what you know and trust.

Then there's everybody else. Don't be trusting a one of them…and keep a weather eye on the ones you do. Especially kin." I knew he wasn't referring to me none, but instead the uncle that we never mentioned. Man had gone and become a lawyer, doing divorces and ambulances and the like. Too fancy for me and Pap.

Them folks on Mercury had gone and made theyselves into "other folk" and there was no way was I gonna even bother to be warning them if they wasn't gonna come on out and help like they was supposed to.

I hit the fire button.

And them mass drivers fired off like lasers into the night. The contrails cleared the edge of Mercury-shadow a few hundred klicks from the drivers and the solar wind whipped the exhaust away like a snowstorm in a hurricane whips ice up a polar bear's behind. Shudders must be running all round that rock. It'd be probably a decade before the planet even rotated one extra turn per orbit, and it was gonna be a rough ride down on there 'til then. Low, pulsin' vibrations that would jar against your brain just below hearing for every hard-Earther there. That'd show them folk for leavin' a lady alone on such a dirty job.

Man, firing off them drivers sure lit up the comm channels in some serious kinda hurry. But no chance I'd be answering them ground-pounders after they'd ignored me all these weeks. I set the *Elsie* down as sweet and polite as the fluff off a cottonwood tree, just at the main port.

They'd have tore the airlock off the hinges trying to welcome me, if it had hinges.

They was shoutin' and cussin'. And I was getting set to shout and cuss right back at 'em.

Pap and his quick hand with a hazel switch had always taught me to mind my language, but they was temptin' me something fierce.

That was 'bout the time I noticed my message queue. I'd written my arrival message, just forgot to hit the old Send key. I deleted that message real quiet-like and calmed down after I'd ripped them only one or two times up and down 'stead a the ten or twenty I'd planned on.

So, none of us was too happy by the time I got into that there base and I sure needed a beer and then a good man between my legs.

Or maybe other way 'round would be okay, too.

Now a beer out on Europa, that's somethin'. The water is different, soft kinda and sweet. Martian ice beer at the Low-Gee Lounge, that was somethin' else too, so dark you could practically chew it. Here on Mercury station, sitting in a back booth that had clearly been stolen from some drive-in diner back in the Age of Democracies right down to the flickerin' lights and squidgy music, they served recycled pale ale lighter than corn mash wort afore it was cooked.

And the walls were the same pale color as the ale. Since when was pee-yellow primer a friendly color? Up-system the Plas always got painted. First thing. On Mercury it just matched their sad excuse for a beer.

Now the waste processors on my ship always made water taste just fine, but these folks here sure as shootin' didn't get it clean before makin' this Mercury…pee-water—there was just no nicer word for it.

The waiter come over to offer me another, but the chances of my keeping this stodge down at all was pretty slim as it was, so I only ordered one more. Needed some buffer against the subsonics rippling through the rock and right up the old mastoid.

I watched him walk away. Now that was a cute behind. Not many men wore them tight pants and even fewer should, but on this one it sure was nice.

Course, I'd never been much of a one for the pretty boys. Always been partial to the ones what had a chance of winning a wrestlin' match agin me, always liked a challenge in my bed.

But this one.

Somethin' about him. He moved smooth and graceful in the one-third gee as he drew my half-liter.

He was running the joint and I was about the only one left. The other five tables were deserted except for one loser snoozin' it off two tables over. Everyone else had cleared out and headed for their racks. Not one decent man among 'em had offered to buy a lady a drink or invite her into their bed.

I'd have to warn Jen next time I saw her.

Mercury men.

Just solar stupid jerks.

But that waiter was a comin' back. From the short buzz cut, down past that fresh face and clean sweater, I focused on them hips and thought about 'em. The little bit of an apron for holding a bar rag and some credits looked kinda like a tool belt if I squinted right. Somethin' 'bout a man's hips and a toolbelt… they was nice thoughts I was thinkin'. Course a pretty boy like that might not pack much of a punch, but my options were gettin' slim unless I was interested in Mr. Passed Out.

I glanced over. He was droolin' on the table. I turned back to that waiter in his heavy red sweater, so bright it made my eyes swim a bit it did. And them tight pants just hangin' there so nice.

"Hey, good-lookin'. How's 'bout you'n'me go check out the 'commodations in this place?" Not one a my smoothest lines, but a girl can get away with just askin' sometimes, so I jus' asked.

The waiter set the mug on the table and stared right at me. Now them is some of the bluest eyes I ever did see. They looked right through me into the back of my head. I couldn't even blink. It was like I was already laid out bare before him. I could feel my whole body tightening up with anticipation. I might just have to reconsider my policy of avoiding the pretty boys.

"Sure." His voice had a throaty quality that wasn't pretty boy at all. It was pure, lion, king of the pride, sex. Like a sleek panther just dying to leap down on ya and lay waste. Well I was ready for some leapin' myself.

I slugged back the brew and was outta there with my hand around his waist faster'n you could low orbit 'round a space rock. My ship was just across the hall and down a few steps, this base was so small you couldn't get lost if you were a lousy ladybug. I'd go crazy as a revenooer inside a week, and I was used to months alone in my rig which wasn't so big to begin with, even if you counted the cargo space.

I cycled the lock behind us and slammed into him. He wrapped his arms round my neck and rammed his sweet tongue about half down my throat. I grabbed his pretty behind that barely filled my hand. But it were as nice and hard as any I'd ever had the chance to test.

Now this was clearly one pretty boy who

worked out, slender or no, and I could sure appreciate that. I think I fell in love at that moment with his tongue and mine wrestlin' for ground back and forth. I never felt that way for no man. Sure they was fun. Catch 'em, ride 'em 'til they was done in, and let 'em go: just like Pap and his fish. He never kept more'n me and he could eat.

"Weren't right to catch more," he'd say. "Neighbors want some fish, they can catch 'em on their own." Pap was always real clear about everyone doin' their own part.

I wasn't solar stupid. I knowed that's all them men was good for anyway.

But the way this pretty boy made me feel, I was glad the gravity was so light or my knees'd be gone and I'd be down on the deck plating. He dug eager fingers into my big melons and toyed with them until *I* was the one crazier'n a revenooer man.

Finally with a roar like some wild beast, comin' from someplace deep inside me, I sure didn't know where, I flipped him onto my shoulder and dragged him back to my rack. I pulled off his sweater and we slammed back together.

Now that was when I noticed somethin' funny, other than being in love of a sudden and all. We fit together good, but we fit together different. There was more keepin' us apart than just my massive melons.

Next time I got a chance, I looked down. Surprise me like an ice hunter finding a swimming hole on Old Luna with a slide and divin' board all built in. That pretty boy had breasts of his own.

I looked back into them blue eyes. They regarded me with that look-down-into-your-soul-like-you-couldn't-lie-to-nohow kinda look.

I went and looked back down at that nice chest and them natural-born decorations that was standing up so nice. They was right pretty ones, all perky they was, with the cutest little nipples just tight as could be. I slid a hand around from that nice firm behind and reached under that little bar apron. Sure enough there weren't no male equipment there neither.

My pretty boy was a pretty girl.

Well, that was sure news to me.

Then she leaned in and kissed me and my knees did go out. She took me down on the decking and pinned me there with them strong, sweet lips a hers like there was no tomorrow. At least not one that I'd ever live to see. No, ma'm. I took a fresh hold of her tight behind as she rode against me and I pulled her in hard.

Why I'd never thought to look at the pretty ones before was sure beyond me.

Just solar stupid, I guess.

Intro to: Moon Shine

Now readin' my stories you might think it was all smooth sailing and merry times drivin' a Class Four hull 'cross the Up'n'up. But that would be like moonshinin' without a revenooer man or blowed out coils. And the cut from the still would be all hearts (that's the best of the liquor), with no heads nor tails (which are harsh and hard and need another cookin'), never mind that first runout of foreshots that, if a beginner is foolish enough to chug it back anyway, can make ya go blind.

Sometimes driving in the Up'n'up has some serious challenges and y'all gotta be able to figure out all them things that ain't in no manual…and sure ain't in no training them Earth Comm folk ever thought up.

Jen told me 'bout the time she found a stowaway on board. Couldn't figure out where all her supplies was goin' so fast—half her whisky, she's a whisky kinda gal—was gone 'fore she'd been a but a couple days out of orbit. Then the man what had stowed away decided that he wanted everything else for hisself too, includin' Jen. She didn't take too kindly to that and now Jupiter has a new moon, lessen his orbit has finally decayed and he's burned up. He sure burned up Jen some, she was right peeved about running dry a month before hitting Titan.

Course Jen is a creative type gal and the way she finally solved that problem is in this here story, too.

Or the air leak I spent three days huntin' for and worrying if I was gonna ever see old Pap or my best friend Jen ever again, that turned out to be the failure of that measly little fail-safe valve in the privy. Finally figured it out when I felt a bit more wind than usual whilst my bladder was clearing off some excess beer it had got a hold of. That were a messy job to be fixing, I can tell you. Bad as digging a fresh hole for moving the outhouse and accidentally striking an old hole which weren't marked so clear from before.

I won't be talkin' no more about that, not in any story. Still gives me the shudders every time I sit down to do my business.

But I'm still flyin' and I'm still writin' 'cause Jen says these tales is good and all.

Writin' ain't like 'shinin'. There you can always tell if'n it's quality. Pap don't even need no thermometer nor hydrometer no more. He just knows when to change out the jug, what to toss, what to sell, and the best part of the heart-cut to keep for just the family.

I'm writing, but 'til I see Jen laughing at 'em, I got no idea if I'm doing good or not.

Guess I am, so that's why I wrote this one. Ain't nothing better'n your best friend's laugh.

MOON SHINE

It had been an awful long climb up the old gravity well from Mercury Station to Europa Station. My rig was almost as tired as I was from sitting for so long at them controls.

Not that there was all that many places to sit in a Class Four. You got your command chair. Sometimes I'd sit in the copilot chair—not that a Class Four needed a copilot, but it offered a change in the scenery. Well, a little bit. You get a choice of two chairs at the food dispenser and a bunk that can change into a couch. The other bunk wasn't usable as I'd converted that room into my beer keg storage space.

So, as I said, awful long climb and my tush was way past tired.

Earth Comm was always in such a darned rush that a girl could barely scratch the old itch before bein' assigned some wild new plan. Never should have signed with Planetary Engineering, them people didn't have no idea about what was going on up-system. Or down-system for that matter. You'd think that if a girl had just spent three months busting her behind on Mercury, there mighta been something that needed doin' closer by than Jupiter.

But I didn't mind all that much, it kept me in space where I like being and also this girl enjoyed being kept comfortable in beer money even when something broke down.

'Til now.

The climb from Mercury all the way out to Jupiter's orbit had taken its toll and the *Elsie* had more problems than her itchy commander who'd just spent four months' solitary confinement in a box no bigger than a Luna rolligon without a single soul in grabbing distance.

I set me up the old Jupiter atmosphere

aero-brake. I roared up from the inner system with enough speed to send me to the stars, rode a hard curve down into the methane and hydrogen and other kinda stuff that Jupiter calls atmosphere, bleeding off speed and creating heat, and then me and the *Elsie* climbed all nice and slow up to the orbit of Europa.

Except the moon wasn't nowhere it was supposed to be.

Now there's something about them orbital mechanics that's kinda important…they don't change much. The Earth is gonna take a year to get around Mama Sol every time. And Jupiter, she'll mosey her fine behind through a full orbit when it good and well pleases her. But she'll do it regular as can be.

Now them little moons what orbit about Jupiter do the same thing, just like clockwork.

Except I'm looking out my nav port and there ain't no moon nowhere in sight. Last I checked there was sixty-something moons they'd found around Jupiter. Though why you'd be calling a space rock less than a kilometer across a moon instead of a rock is way past this girl's understanding. You'd have to be asking them fools at Earth Comm and this girl sure wasn't about to.

First, askin' anything of Earth was like as not to bury a girl in no end of paperwork and second, you'd never be able to understand their answer anyways.

Third was more important though, at least to me personal-like. My comm gear went down somewhere around about when I crossed Mars orbit and I was hoping to have some service chick more nimble than me crawl into *Elsie's* guts and fix things up right. I'd tried it, but no way had the access ports been built for big gals like me. Some pencil-neck male with no breasts or hips had designed the access port. The only way I was getting in to where the comm gear was broke, was with an ax.

But it was the old Catch-22. The nearest service was on Europa, but my comm gear would sure be useful getting' there in the first place. And it didn't help none that the radar dish went missing when some asteroid with a whole lotta attitude swung by and took off with it while I was crossing the Belt. I will admit to being glad it hadn't decided to go through the cabin just for giggles along its way.

Couldn't go out to fix it neither. My suit was fine, except I couldn't find the left glove. Musta left it on Mercury after getting that nice, nice all-night send-off that I got. Wasn't too clearheaded when I took my leave. All I'd been good for was to punch in the initial burn and then just sleep the first two days with a smile on my face.

I was past Venus before I missed that glove. And my spare was in the cargo bay, which had no pressure. I wasn't going out into no pressure, freezin'-your-behind-off-even-in-a-suit kinda cold without my glove, not if I had any interest in living, which I did. And because stupid Earth Comm had ordered such a long jump, I couldn't afford the air to jazz up the cargo bay for one lousy glove. Not lessen I wanted to be breathing space by the time I hit Jupiter orbit.

So here I was, hangin' 'round the backside of Jupiter, cruising just pretty as could be, but there was no moon awaitin' for me. This set me a fair problem, other than being alone too long and all.

Europa ain't no little one- or two-klick wide space rock. She was number three of the big four around Jupiter. I mean to be sayin', she ranked in the top twenty in the whole solar system for size including the planets and Mama Sol.

Stories said that old Mister Galileo had spotted this moon hisself all the way from Earth when he thought of using his brand-new telescope to look at heavenly bodies farther away than in a building across the street. And I was a durn sight closer'n he was. I should be able to see it just fine.

But it wasn't there.

You'd think that losing a heavenly body only a third smaller than the planet Mercury would be a hard thing to do, but space gets awful big and dark especially as you move up-system. *Elsie's* computer said I was in the right place, but the moon sure wasn't. But neither could I imagine someone moving Europa to someplace new anytime recent. Even without my radio for the last two months, I woulda knowed about that.

What with all that water in her frozen-over oceans, she was the most valuable piece of property in the system after Earth herself. Nobody'd mess with that anyways, not even if we could figure out how. Don't think even the Planetary Engineering people is that kinda foolish. But that little moon sure wasn't showing her face; not that I could see.

Not quite sure what to do about this, I drew myself a beer before settlin' in to think about things. One thing I did know for sure, I'd better hurry. I knocked the old keg with my foot to test her, this was right near my last beer.

Now being out of beer was its own problem. One right serious in its nature to my way of thinking.

I didn't usually figure my stock so close. I always kept plenty aboard to jump Earth to Jupiter or even the big leap from Jupiter to Saturn, but Mercury to Jupiter had stretched the old limits. And even after I'd helped them out fixing up their brewing equipment at Mercury, it still wasn't what you'd call good.

Also, the fees for taking resources off the planet was fierce. Mercury Central kept claiming they didn't have any water to spare. If you didn't pee it out, you wasn't supposed to take it back off the god-forsaken rock they called home. So, as I wasn't headed out to Pluto or Charon, I'd only filled the water tanks to half to keep my costs down. Even with that, I'd been counting on hitting the Europa LaunchPub real soon and getting some of that fine Deep-ice Lager they brew there.

I'd tried cooking beer in transit, but it never worked out. Just a logistical nightmare it was. Some places didn't want to let go of their hops or wheat. And one bad batch could leave a girl seriously stranded. So, it was easier to stock up on the finished product at the latest planetfall—unlessen it was Mercury. If that purty gal what had given me the fine send-off hadn't a slipped me a keg or two on the sly, I'd be some kinda desperate right 'bout now.

Asides, I liked the variety as I worked around the system. But now this girl was heading into a crisis of a more personal nature.

I needed a beer, a man, and a moon, but I wasn't going to find them in that order.

Thankfully the Mercury brew was lame enough that I couldn't get too lost in the nostalgia about my send-off and all. That, and I'd worn them memories pretty shiny over the four-month-alone trip out here to where the sun didn't shine so much. Way past time to get some fresh memories loaded aboard while I was seeing to things. I mean as long as I was makin' lists and all.

So: no comm, no nav, and no moon. That moon was the real problem. Old Europa was the only one with more than a science station on her, and she was the only one with beer. So even if I could find one of them other moons, it didn't excite me so much. I was betting none of them others would have a new nav dish or comm gear that I was needing.

Where could a moon like Europa get herself off to? She's got an orbit just a million-and-a-half kilometers across. And she should be right there a couple thousand klicks off my port bow. But I didn't have nothin' excepting my eyeballs to pin her down with. The old nav computer couldn't get me any closer without a radar image and that wasn't coming without my left glove and a new radar dish that I didn't have anyway.

I checked the old port-glass again, but there wasn't nothing to see out there asides from big Jupiter being all grouchy-like she was, a tiny point of the old Sun 'bout the size of the tip of my pinkie-nail held out at arm's length, and a whole mess of stars. I watched the scenery through that beer and the next without spotting a single thing moving against the background.

The old tank sputtered dry when I went for just one more pint. That set me onto a whole other track of thinking. There weren't a lot of ways to make alcohol with what I had on the ship. I ran through my inventory in my mind and by the time I was done, I'd come up with exactly no ideas.

So I set into thinking of what others had come up with when faced with such dire circumstances.

Jen on the *Lucy* had once raided the medical supplies outta her cargo bay. She'd come into Titan drunk as a skunk. As a side benefit, she sure wasn't going to ever cough again with the amount of syrup she'd slurped up. That didn't help me none as Planetary Engineering had me making this run empty because they was in such an all-fired hurry. Hadn't even told me what it was. They just said go, so this gal went.

There was Old Johnson, he'd gotten real creative. He'd found a way to crack rocket fuel into alcohol. It wasn't the safest thing to be doing, but we all gave him points for creativity and daring. Right up 'til he was shifting a big old highly-radioactive asteroid into a close-Earth orbit for mining and he accidentally blew hisself up before he got it all the way stopped. The explosion had been so spectacular that it had shattered the asteroid. Let's just say that the chunks coming in had put a real crimp in the viability of New York City for the next thousand or so half-lives of Strontium-90.

Down on Earth they was upset by that something fierce, never mind that the place had emptied out long ago, what with the ocean covering Manhattan since forever. It was just another marine park was all, but the stink and whining was still goin' on years later.

"Git over it," my Pap woulda snapped at them. But I wasn't as daring as my Pap and just kept my thoughts to myself and any other spacers I happened to be jawing with.

Crackin' rocket fuel wasn't gonna be workin' for me anyway. They'd changed fuels since then and nobody, not even a smart gal like me, had come up with a way to recook Gel-fuel into anything other than more Gel-fuel.

Made me think of my old Pap.

He was good at two things. He loved his fishing and he loved his still. We was always flat broke, but we ate well and, everyone in the county agreed, we drank well. He made as fine a corn liquor as anybody anywhere, though I'd grown to prefer beer myself. Hard to program a three-planet sling-shot orbit on 'shine, especially Pap's. However, you could use his brew to fire a rocket if you ever needed.

He'd given me a case as a gift when I got the Elsie and I'd come right close to punching her smack into Luna on my first flight. Mighta mentioned that already, but it's kinda worth mentioning again 'cause that flight sorta changed my thinkin' 'bout my drinkin'.

After that, and finishing the case except for one bottle I'd kept back for medicinal purposes, I'd switched over to beer. Hard for a girl to get drunk on the stuff, the old bladder moves it along too fast, but it loosens things up nice.

Pap and his old 'shine. He was probably down on the river right now, drunk as two skunks and fishing. I checked the clock. I kept it set to Earthtime. The folks down at Planetary Engineering, despite all the bees up their behinds, hated being called in the middle of the night. Pap was only a couple hours off from Earthtime, meaning it was the middle of the night there too. So unless he was fishing by moonshine…

That's when I started into thinkin' I just might know where that sneaky little moon Europa had gone. I knocked back the last of my beer and went and peered out the old window again. Had to squint a bit to bring them old stars back inta focus. I cleaned the inside of the glass which didn't help as much as I'd been hoping.

Seemed to me that moon *had* to be right there smack-dab in front of me.

But if I shifted orbit in one direction and she was in the other, I'd be in some kinda trouble finding the extra reaction mass to change my mind.

I was looking toward the sun.

And that old moon was closer to the sun than me, just not in front of her. That meant all the light was a-shining on one face of Europa and I was a staring at t'other. I was staring up her backside that was as dark as space hisself.

No question 'bout the gender of space as

he was always trying to nail your behind, and not in no good way.

So that's why I wasn't seeing none of the moon. She was shining on the exact other side.

Now what I had to do was figure how to see her shinin' face so as I could find her. Took a bit of doin', but I got her figured and headed on in a couple days later once I had it sure.

Jen and the *Lucy* was in as well when I finally made it. So we was sitting in the back of the Europa LaunchPub, each with our own pitcher of Deep-ice Lager. Smooth and sweet.

The place was 'bout half full and already plenty loud—a real nice change from my own singin' out in the depths of the Up'n'up. The LP was one of only three bars in space big enough to support a live band. LaunchPub's band sure weren't good, but they was loud and their music made your feet want to jiggle about just for the fun of it, so none of us complained much about the not good part. 'Sides, them other two bands is even worse.

The long Plas bar was loaded up with just about every kind of space-jock and science geek you could imagine. By starting in early, we'd scored one of the cozy, raised circular booths that offered a grand view of the mayhem. I told Jen some about how folks got stupider the closer to the sun and she told me about finishing off the L2 Habitat and then gettin' finished off real nice up against the main command desk. Seems the command crew gave her a fine send-off in special thanks for her hard workin' an' all.

By the time we was sorta caught up some, it was off-shift for most of them Europa workers and the LaunchPub was packed way past full. The mob was so tight and so loud that you couldn't tell if they was dancing or talking or fighting. It was just a glorious throbbing mass of humanity which was a serious relief after four months in my solitary can climbing up-system.

The best part was the way the men was eying us. Now Jen, she's a pretty little thing. Tough as nails, but right nice to look at. When she crooks her pinky, they came a-running. Me, well, it would take about three of Jen to make one of me. Not that I let myself go, I was just a big gal and that scared a lot of the men off.

Which was fine with me.

I wasn't one to be wantin' any city-boy types in my rack. I wanted someone worth a good wrestle, and the LaunchPub had plenty of interesting possibilities. I'd been flying in the Up'n'up for nigh on five years and there was more women comin' in. Leastwise they told us there was, but hadn't seen 'em yet. Story was that most of 'em wanted those cushy-type jobs in the new Tycho Up'n'up Admin building. By the time y'all got up-system, there was still five boys for every girl. Just sayin' that this whole "Women in Space" movement wasn't gonna be hurtin' my chances none anytime soon.

So, for now, we was glad to sit and let them boys watch us while we worked on our beers, caught up on old times, smelled sweat that wasn't our own, and jiggled the old feet to the cranking music.

"Took me some to figure out what was a-going on," I shouted at Jen after we finished comparing all the details about our fine send-offs.

Never was a gal liked hearin' the details of that kinda send-off as much as my best pal Jen. But we'd finally run that one dry for now and I was tellin' her 'bout my most recent adventure.

"I mean there I was only a couple thousand klicks from the nearest pub," I poured myself a fresh glass. "But I couldn't see a darn thing."

"What did you do?" Jen's brow knitted as much as a girl's could for being well into her second pitcher of brew.

"I finally figured out what was wrong 'cause of my old Pap. I'd done a slingshot aero-brake, ducking down around the Jupiter's backside to bleed off my flight speed, and come around the other side facing into the sun. Problem was, I'd come up right behind Europa."

With a slight tipping of her glass, Jen pointed out a couple nice-looking boys what were eyeing us from the end of the bar. Real nice. She glanced over at me and I nodded, knowing I needed to be finishing up my story right quick. A problem I wouldn't be minding a bit.

Jen crooked her pinkie the way she does and the two boys lit up like sunshine theyselves and begun working their way over to our table all casual-like.

"The sun was on the *far* side of the moon," I shouted over the music, but was aiming my smile on the bigger guy. Broad-shoulders, big-callused hands, and powerful arms that said he worked hard for a living. Looked like he played hard too. Just what this girl was needing.

His smile came back hot as a reentry burn. This was gonna be good.

"So I was looking at the backside of the moon, away from the sunlight. No shine of the sun off Europa's surface ice for me to spot her by." Around the backside like I'd been, a starin' toward Mama Sol, even the glow off Jupiter wasn't enough to show me where the moon was at.

Me and Jen both knew that Europa's orbit about Jupiter was 'bout eighty-five hours. Jen caught on soon as I told her—she always was the smart one—'bout how I'd figured I only had to wait about a day for me and the moon to drift around old Lady Jupiter and into the sunlight so as I could spot her. Europa had a nice tight orbit, just like these two boys closing in on our table.

"So what did you do while you waited?" We shifted in shoulder to shoulder making room for the two boys who was sliding into our booth. It was just like old times when I first met Jen. We'd done the same thing back in Tycho pickin' up our first pair of men together all them years back. We done shared a smile for old times, but now wasn't a moment to be wasted doin' more.

"Well…" The boy offered his hand. Instead I snagged him by the back of the neck and kissed him hard.

He only hesitated for a moment, then he leaned in serious-like, one of his hands already massaging my massive melons ever so nice. This was gonna be serious bunches a fun.

Me and Jen both broke off for just a second and I told her the end.

"I had this one medicinal bottle left of Pap's old moonshine. By the time I was done with it…" I shrugged.

"The moon was shining!" Jen always had a great laugh.

I joined in.

Then we both turned to more important-like matters.

Intro to: Double Down

There's times for workin' hard in the Up'n'up and there's times for just sittin' back and havin' a good jaw. This story's about one of those latter-type times.

Now Pap was never a gamblin' man. He didn't believe in it none and taught me that with a switch, right after finding me more'n halfway through losin' a game of strip poker with Jake when I was thirteen and him sixteen. Taught me he didn't believe in gamblin' none for his kin neither. Pap never had to explain something twice. Or even once. He'd just show his girl where she went wrong and leave it up to me to mend my ways. Pap made his point and I never touched no cards or other gamblin' again.

"Never bet on nothing but a sure thing," he said when he was done showin' me the error of my ways. "Even then, make sure you're moving the shell-game cups youself." An' he stomped off like he did whenever he'd needed to cut a switch and use it some. It hurt me, but I know it hurt him too and he always had to go off for a while and calm down some after.

As to me and Jake and things having nothing to do with cards, well, that was a sure thing makin' him an easy bet. We discovered the hayloft worked just fine as long as we was quiet and didn't disturb Pap none.

But, even if it kinda hurts me to say, there be times when Pap doesn't know everything. That were a real shock to me I can tell you.

When I done told Jen one night that I don't gamble she looked at me kinda funny. We was wetting the old whistles at the Low-Gee Lounge on Mars waitin' for a fresh load of finished iron to be loaded up 'cause Ganymede was wantin' some. Nothing much to do, so we was just shootin' the breeze.

"You gamble, girl." She said it all indignant-like.

"No, ma'am, Jen. Not this girl." Jen always laughed big when I called her ma'am. Not sure why.

"What about that one time? Way up-system?"

I thought me through a beer or two and knew she was right. There was this one time I had to take a bet, a big old one. And it paid off, and I gotta admit all honest-like, it weren't no sure thing.

I tole this story to a passel of science types I was supposed to be movin' about the Up'n'up and I've tried to write it down the same way I tole it to them.

They didn't seem to take to it kindly, not sure why.

I thought it was a good story at the time. Still do.

So does Jen, so here it be.

DOUBLE DOWN

We be sittin' about smack on Saturn's orbit. The only problem bein' that Saturn is on the far side of the solar system at the moment. I shoulda thought about that some more beforehand, I'll admit. We sure as shootin' wouldn't be in the crapper like we is if I had. That reminds me of somethin' kinda funny that happened to me once. Y'all might like this story.

You know, sometimes a girl just has to roll the dice, even when she knows the chance of hitting boxcars is one in thirty-six. 'Course I hadn't thought the odds of rolling snake eyes that time was like thirty-five chances in thirty-six if'n I wasn't gonna hit boxcars.

I shoulda. Mighta thought it, if I hadn't had me quite so much fine brew and such a nice, nice arrival at Europa Station after a long-as-a-back-country-winter solo haul up from Mercury. That piece a nice had kept me in my rack for days, him just waiting for me every time I turned around. Sometimes a girl gets lucky, and I was feeling very lucky.

That luck musta gone to my head 'cause that's when I told my bosses something that really didn't have much chance of coming out good no matter how you calculated them odds. As old Pap used to say before wandering down to the stream with his jug of 'shine and his fishing pole:

"That was damn stupid, girl." Pap always was the smart one.

Wisht I coulda asked him for some of his advice, but by the time I was in trouble the sun was a tiny little dot way down-system and he never was much of a one for things like phones. He didn't like it so much when anyone other than his 'shine customers could find him. No, not one bit.

S'pose I should back up and explain what I done and how I come to be out here.

Y'all know that I drive the *Elsie* for a living.

No, the *Elsie* ain't named for no cow. Don't get why folks keep asking that. Named her for my ma. No, she ain't name for no cow neither. Now hush so I can get on with it.

The *Elsie,* that's my ship not my ma, is a Class Four transport and constructor ship; maybe not the best in the fleet, but I swear by one a them old saints that she's sure the toughest.

Anyways, me and the Elsie we been together ever since I lifted off the old rock, nigh on five years back. The thing you Earthers still don't get is that a lifetime spent drivin' 'cross the Up'n'up sure ain't about freedom and liberty, not if you sign on with Earth Comm. And even if you're a private flyer, Earth Comm will still be bossing y'all around just 'cause that's their job. Me personal, I got no problem with them doing that. Not so much as I'd do more than complainin' with my fellow pilots over a pitcher or two of good brew.

Oh, there is some who gets a bit hot under the collar, Tank McCaw comes to mind. Earth

Comm got him all het up so he dropped ten thousand tons of nickel ore asteroid from high Earth orbit down on top their headquarters one night.

He did wait until they went home like they always done. And like was anyone gonna really miss Boise, Idaho? Such a hoopla you never heard. Tank got in all sorts of trouble for that one, happen to know he's still staying up-system doin' odd jobs where they can't be findin' him. Last I heard Earth Comm had built their new building down in some caves or other, though they wasn't telling which ones.

As I said, I got no real problem with Earth Comm. But why in all creation I signed with Planetary Engineering is way past reckoning. When I did that one, Pap didn't even tell me how stupid I was bein'. Instead, he just shook his head and muttered something about, "Kids. Always gotta learn the hard way."

PE folks are crazier than a blue tick hound what caught his own scent then can't find where it's coming from. Right before this story I'm a-thinking of, they'd hauled my sorry behind straight-shot from Mercury up to Jupiter orbit in a single pull without any cargo along the way. Once't they got me there, none of them could remember why they'd sent me in the first place. Now my tush ain't small like some little pretty girl, as I work for a livin', but I sure didn't appreciate being left to sit on it any more than the old *Elsie* did. She's always happiest when plying her trade.

'Sides, just sittin' there was building up my bar tab and not my pocketbook. Pap was always real strict about that: money up front for his 'shine was the only way he done business all these years.

So that brings me up to my nice welcome at Europa station. And I wasn't complaining 'bout neither the welcome or the brew; LaunchPub claims the best brew in the system and I ain't found better.

While Jeffrey, the one who was givin' me the nice welcome, was continuing nice, he was gettin' kinda predictable. Ol' Jeffrey is definitely a T-and-A man. As I got plenty of both, he was right happy when I picked him outta the crowd. And while he was doin' his best to show me just how happy he was about that, he didn't have a lot a variety. I don't need no carnival show to keep my attention focused on such things, but by the second night I knew he was a predictable soul with far too little of that creativity stuff flowing through his veins to keep me happy more'n through the week. Maybe two.

So, I did this crazy-dumb thing one night. I wrote me a message to old PE. Don't remember it too clear, as Jeffrey and I had pretty much closed the LaunchPub, which they did only once a day for an hour afore breakfast to hose the place down. It went something like this:

Use my behind or lose it. Twenty-four hours or I'm callin' Transport.

On that first roll of the dice I figured I had me a good bet. There ain't nothing that Planetary Engineering hates worse than Ore Transport. OT is just like you'd expect: long, hard, boring-as-can-be hours, but the pay was sweet 'cause Earth Comm thought pushing around a bunch a lazy asteroids was more dangerous than drivin' acrost all sorta variable-type places. PE was losing pilots to Ore Transport all the time. Me and my pal Jen had talked about it some, but PE jobs typical keeps a gal closer to the pubs and a fresh supply of men.

Asides, me, personal, I liked the variety of PE work even if they was crazier than loons. And *Elsie* was a constructor ship and I wasn't gonna leave her to the evil clutches of whatever ham-handed hard-rocker that PE coaxed aloft to fly her once I moved on. We've kinda gone and gotten attached over the years.

So, I figured PE would find some good use for us before I totally run out of any use for Jeffrey. I like to leave a man hanging with some potential of interest in him, in case I find myself back somewhere needin' a dose of company.

It was fifty minutes down-system for my signal as Earth was in opposition at the moment, swinging her fine behind through space on the far side of her orbit on the other side of the sun. Fifty minutes back up, and I figured at least a dozen hours in between, 'cause sure as the sun don't set in space, they never do anything without every single fool signing off on something.

So me and Jeffrey, we was waiting when the LaunchPub reopened and settled in to watch the crazy antics of the early morning boozies and all them nightshifters standing down for the day and trying to work up some extra rowdy.

A pitcher for each of us, and we was all set.

A hundred and three minutes after I sent my cute little message, I received a sealed packet. A hundred in transit and three settin' up to ruin my life.

I ain't never received no sealed packet before. Heard of 'em, we all have. High priority and so hush-hush you can't even open 'em while docked at a station. The cover code said to kick Elsie with a hard burn further up-system, then the packet would unseal an hour out. At a full tenth-of-gee burn, we'd only be a little ways out, but we'd be moving at near enough four kilometers a second. Tough to turn back from that.

I thought it was kind of exciting.

But I swear I could hear Pap's voice as if he was the one serving me my last pitcher at the LaunchPub, "You're young and stupid, girl."

Turned out Pap was right again.

I made sure that my kegs and larder were filled. I did take the time for one last tumble with old Jeffrey. Not a thing new, but he sure did know how to make a girl feel appreciated. I'd be feelin' his hands on me for some bit of a while.

Now I kinda understood the excitement that them what plays games of chance must feel and didn't care if them dice was a little bit loaded.

That packet unsealed herself an hour out, just as promised.

But I hadn't expected PE to repaint them dice entire after I rolled 'em!

Unlike Earth Comm, I knew exactly where Planetary Engineering had slimed the surface of the old home planet and if I had a couple thousand tons of heavy asteroid ore handy, I'd be kicking it right down on their heads even if it would destroy Pap's favorite fishing stream. It said that I should:

Proceed up-system to MPD 134340. Construct tracking and locator beacon type B14 and install at either pole.

I thought about tackling my first keg until I just calmed down some; but if I was heading all the way out to Pluto—for any fool what lived crawling up and down the system knew that the Minor Planet Designation of Pluto was 134340, mostly 'cause Earth Comm couldn't seem to figure how to spell "Pluto" in their messages—I needed to think some things through. Forty days at max acceleration and another forty deceleration; eighty days to Pluto, each way burnin' the whole way. Even with full kegs, there was no way I had six months' supply aboard. If I did, the *Elsie* wouldn't fly, she'd wallow. Just not enough room in the living spaces, and beer ain't so good once it freezes in the old cargo bay.

Now this here was a serious situation, so I drew at least one beer just to lubricate the old thinking parts.

First I had to wonder why Planetary Engineering wanted those beacons, it wasn't as if Pluto was gonna go off wandering on his own. I mean he might have been a god and all back in Greek times and a dog in Disney times, but for as long as anyone knew, he been a frozen lump who'd briefly been a planet.

Maybe them beacons was so aliens could find us better. Personal, I didn't want to meet up with nobody what was forced to detour and slow down for Pluto only to find nothing there but a couple of hundred-meter tall towers, blinking brainlessly on and off on every frequency there was in that whole EM spectrum. It was just rude.

Pap never would have stood for such a thing. But then Pap had also tole me, "Never bite the hand holdin' yer meal ticket."

I wanted to ask him if Planetary Engineering counted, but he was kinda far off to call now.

By my second beer, I wasn't any wiser on what PE was up to. Downright inscrutable is what them folks is. Finally decided it was a waste of further beer and turned back to my original problem.

No matter how I figured my rations, I was coming up two months shy, and I didn't like the thought of rationing my beer supply. I had four months' worth aboard. It was time to get creative.

Turning back wasn't an option. For one thing, if I did, they'd fire me and I'd have to pay for my own reaction mass and bar tab after that. Didn't like either of them ideas, not even one little bit.

So me and *Elsie* was going to MPD 134340 even if it were a dry run.

Now I'd been given a garbage dice-roll. Like Planetary Engineering thought the way to keep me out of Ore Transport's hands was to isolate me for six months all by myself to cruise the outer reaches. Hard to make a comeback from a position like that. But I was doing some hard thinking.

Problem was thinking took fuel. By the time I hit crossed Saturn's orbit, I was already through the first keg…or maybe it was two by then. Anyway, it wasn't good. I did what I could to minimize my time at Pluto, pre-fabricating the towers from stock material I'd kept in the *Elsie's* cargo bay. Didn't have enough air to pressurize the bay for the whole trip, so I did most of it with suit work. Suit time had a nice bonus rate in my contract, so that was good.

It was half past Neptune when I decided to really gamble. There's times you just have to bet it all on one roll. Took a whole lot of thinkin' fuel to plan it out, but I got her figured.

I'd be hittin' atmo with less than a keg remaining, but that was the key.

I was gonna *hit* atmo.

I'd looked me up old Pluto's atmosphere. Thin as could be, but we was talking ethane, just floating there. I'd sweep in low, real low as there ain't much atmo like I said, and scoop up every bit of it that I could. I'd leave the scoop running ethane into the tanks for every minute it took me to plant them two beacons.

Way I figured it, I had plenty of oxygen, just not enough beer. Do you know what happens when you add a single oxygen molecule to ethane? No?

Well, I ain't Pap's daughter if I don't know how to cook up something when I need to. Took me right down to the last three beers in my last keg to figure it out, but I did. I'd scooped up about a ton of ethane. So on the ride back down-system, I cracked her open and slipped in some old oxygen I just happened to have lying about and cooked me some ethanol. Pure drinking alcohol. Two hundred proof, even better than Pap's. When I got back, I sent the old man a bottle an' he told me I done good and he was proud a me. Brought a couple a tears to my eyes I can tell you.

That's how I know we'll get out of this mess too, what with Saturn bein' in the wrong place and all. Planetary Engineering or Lady Luck might roll the dice, but a smart player knows when to double down.

Meanwhile, anyone want a drink? I've still got a couple hundred gallons of the Elsie's finest back in the hold; it freezes up just fine.

Got me mess of thinking to do.

Intro to: 13:33

Now I done told a whole lotta stories about me and *Elsie.* But no matter how I tell 'em, Jen always seems to just be on the sidelines.

But that ain't how a woman and her best friend is, out here in the Up'n'up. You get to dependin' on each other for the little things and the big ones. Tradin' stories when you're feelin' blue. Tradin' men when you find a good one but your assignment has you heading out just as your best friend is headin' in.

In the Up'n'up, we gals have to stick close. Well to some.

I can't argue with what Jen says about

Evgenia. That woman got a chip on her shoulder worse'n any man. She don't drink. She don't share herself with all them eager menfolk, not even when they ask nice. She been at it so long that she still flies a Class Two hull—threatened to ram it into Tycho Central Dome if they tried to decommission it. Spotless, that ship looks factory fresh, but ain't hardly nobody in the yards no more knows how to work on her. Ev is just a stubborn sort. But as she don't drink and all, we don't see much of her in port.

Me and Jen are still the only other gal pilots drivin' 'cross the Up'n'up.

There somethin' about a gal friend that no man can get. He sits with a buddy and he's talkin' about how much he got paid or what sports team won. Sometimes he'd do what he can to cut off his buddy, like if he's trying to get to one of us gals.

Never understood it none.

Pap weren't like that. When we was havin' a bad month 'cause Johnny Law broke up a couple shipments or something, Pap always shared what food we had fair and square.

"You earn it, you get to it eat it."

He didn't share his 'shine so much when

stock was low, but I never held that against him none. He put his heart into making that and it was right important to him.

I guess I'll talk more about being gal friends in a bit. 'Til then, here be a story that's just about me and Jen.

13:33

_13:33_

That's what the clock said when the bang knocked me outta my bunk. The old *Elsie* weren't supposed to be making no bangs and she definitely weren't supposed to be slopping about enough that I needed to sleep in a harness in zero-gee; harnesses was for atmo work 'less a gal minded drifting around some.

Trouble was the old clock had flipped to bright red and added a blaring alarm just in case I had any earwax I was in the mood to be rid of.

Space was a generally silent sorta place

where a girl could dream about what a time she'd had kickin' feet out from under the two boys who'd given her such a fine send-off from The Belt just a couple days back.

The Belt was one of the smallest pubs in the Up'n'up seeing as how it was located on Ceres, deep in the Asteroid Belt. Most folks aimed high above the old Ecliptic Plane when jumping from Mars to Jupiter. But I'd had me some doings out at old Ceres, emergency supplies that them boys over in Ore Transport couldn't get in place despite runnin' back there empty.

Some kinda union thing back on Earth.

Planetary Engineering (that's my kinda folks what fly constructor ships) gotta be the ones t' haul new constructions out to the ore mines. Works fine for me as I like the hazard pay and I like just how few gals there is up there workin' them asteroids. Got me no competition at all really and take my pick of The Belt every time I walked through her swinging doors to order a brew. Never had to pay none either which was real nice of them boys and I always done my best to show how I appreciated them bein' so nice.

But that old clock had my attention pretty

good at the moment. It was counting down in red. Normal-like, it showed the time sync from Earth Comm in cheery green. Now it was red and that worried me a bit right off. And countin' down instead of up which weren't encouragin' at all.

13:20

That sure was *not* s'posed to be how much longer a gal had to live, but that's what the darned thing was telling me.

Then the oxygen alarm kicked in with a sharp bleat. Not a fun way to go, not even a little. That was a seriously bad change to my morning.

Always figured there was two ways death was s'posed to happen.

Instantaneous-like, or close enough so as it didn't matter none. Even if the dying took some time, the event that led to the dying was quick enough that there was no point in minding how it all come about. 'Sides, you'd be too busy worrying 'bout the end to pay any real mind to what else you could be thinking given half a chance.

The other option happened along when some sadistic medico with a passel of glee for a-messing with a girl's gray matter declared, "six months to live."

When the express line to the big check-out happened, you didn't have time to care. In the slow line, maybe a girl had some time to affect the outcome; maybe not, but it would be nice to think there was an option. At least there'd be time to sort of get your shorts on straight and find where your hat had gone afore it was time to do any bucket kickin'. Maybe even get a chance at poppin' that medico a good one in the nose.

Let me tell you, this third option—that was part way in-between with its counting clocks and bleating horns—was not some ideal place to be. It weren't decent for a woman to be sitting on the cold deck in her nightgown and staring at a red timer just counting its little heart out in the wrong direction.

But 12:59 was getting on my nerves. It gave you plenty a time for the thinkin' and not so much for the doin'.

First up? I checked the reason for what was going on. Seems some joker had gone and spilt all of my O2 out into space. There's safeties on that. And safeties on them safeties.

It would take more than a meteor, or even a flock of the little suckers to wipe it all out at once. A big meteor hittin' the old *Elsie* was a like-never kind of rare event and if one a them decided to wander your way, you didn't get no 12:46-between-you-and-check-out-time sorta problem.

Second thing I checked was my beer, but my kegs were still full, except the first one that I might have dented a bit, so that was fine if I could avoid the awkward dying problem. I shed my flannel nightgown, but there being no time for underwear type things, I pulled on my suit bare as I was born—always kinda tricky for a woman my size. I've growed some since then and there be parts what don't like being pinched in suit seals, but I was in a hurry, so I managed.

I powered up the suit's batteries and they was fine too.

Problem was, I wasn't havin' much luck breathin' in the thing. I finally cracked open the face plate, gasped in some of the thinning air in the cabin, and started looking around for what was going on.

Bad news, I shoulda recharged the bottles

after doing a passel of unpressurized cargo bay work. Now I didn't have so much to charge my suit with. That was gonna be a major kind of issue.

It wasn't 'til about 11:03 that I figured I was ready to find out what was really going on. Seriously, out between The Belt on Ceres and the Low-Gee Lounge on Mars, there just wasn't a whole lot supposed to be going on.

I did grab a quick brew and knock it back just in case I was goin' t' meet the old Maker Man. Facing death stone cold sober isn't something this girl ever planned on tryin' out.

Around about 9:34, I considered a third beer, but felt I was running narrow on the old clock ticks. If I lived, I'd have to consider a rig that could fill a beer bulb faster than I had.

I combined activities, and started working through *Elsie's* readouts while I pulled that third brew.

Power? Good.

Fuel? Fine.

Air? Yeah, that was gonna be a major problem.

It wasn't 'til I got way down the old list to "Cargo" that I noticed something peculiar.

Somewhere along the way I'd picked up a quick three-thousand kilotons of cargo. It was the sort of thing I'd expect to remember if I'd done it on purpose. Maybe even if I hadn't. That's all the *Elsie* normally weighed empty. All I was supposed to be carrying was a big old stack of titanium framework; Ceres had a new refinery up and running and Mars dome was wanting it hot and heavy. That load hadn't weighed no three million kilos when I took her aboard or I'd've noticed right off.

At 7:19 I turned on the cargo bay cameras. Practically snorted my fourth beer when I saw the mess in there. It took some doing, but I got enough imaging up to see that there was another ship parked in my cargo bay, at least the front third of one.

Constructor Class Three, a gen back from my *Elsie.* Only knew of two working this space lane: Tiny Tex, who didn't get his name for his two-meter height. If you ever had to meet up with a man under other circumstances, trust me, girls—voice of sad experience here—he should be your last choice. The other one was my best friend Jen on the *Lucy.* I knowed we was best friends 'cause she told me so when we first met.

That possibility cheered me up some. We lifted out of atmo together ten years back, Class of '15. Well, she was Class of '14, but them years merge a bit and don't matter so much here in the Up'n'up. 'Special not when you're best friends. Had us a whole lot of good times since then.

At 6:03, the breathing was already getting tricky, so desperate times, desperate measures and all those kinda sayings: I airlocked into my cargo bay and only remembered to gulp down some air and slap down the old face plate at the last moment.

Got it down, then lost a hoppy burp into the suit. At least the air stayed with me.

I'd just traded 5:46 for about 2:00. I've got a big set a lungs, being the size I am, but being a big gal, I use up the O2 in a right regular fashion so no extra help there.

At 1:30, I'd found the other ship's lock and was glad to see that it was the *Lucy*. I had to kick a bunch of the bent titanium frames aside which took me down to 0:54.

I did look about as I cycled the *Lucy's* lock. Old Jen had punched right in through the side of my *Elsie*. And my cargo doors were about the only thing she hadn't crumpled. She'd blown in through my main O2 system and driven all of the titanium frames through my secondaries just like arrows.

Never was much of a bow and arrow girl myself. Melons the size of mine and strings that snap against the sides of them just ain't the kinda pain this girl wants any part of.

Getting a little woozy, I cracked the old faceplate back open when her airlock was about half pressurized. A good yeasty burp, a couple sharp inhales, and I was ready to find out just what was going on.

Through the inside lock, keeping my suit on just in case, I bumped along to the cockpit.

Jen was there sure enough.

Wearing a suit about half the size of mine, 'cause she was more that size of girl, and strapped into the pilot's chair. She was out cold.

Now Jen is more of a whisky person, and I found a half empty bottle soon enough. Took one snort for myself, then held her nose and squirted a shot down the old gullet. That got her attention right quick.

"Hey there, Jen," I said it polite as could be whilst she coughed and spluttered.

"Hey yourself," she managed, a bit rough.

I got me another drink and then checked her clock. Still green, so no air leaks trying to kill us right off. No fuel leaks trying to blow us up neither. I took that as a good omen. I double-checked—no fuel at all, makin' it not such a good omen. But as she had air and something to drink, I took off my helmet anyways figurin' I'd stay a bit. I did think to plug my suit in for a recharge.

"You're here!" Jen was seeming a little blurry, so I handed her a refill.

"Glad you ain't Tiny Tex."

"I'm glad I'm not, too," Jen nodded and drank. "Sad way to be."

"So, what's up, Jen?"

"Flamer."

That explained that. The old Class Three hulls sometimes had an engine flame kick on and go runaway. Engineering claimed they got that fixed on all the older ships, but us as flew in the Up'n'up knowed better.

Only way to douse it was dump it in an ocean. No ocean handy? You just had to ride it out until your fuel was gone. It put an awful amount a heat in the hot rod and finding a way to stop after it flamed out usually required running into something solid. 'Less of course you wanted a slow trip to the stars because you'd be way past Mama Sol's escape velocity.

"I saw the *Elsie* in the lane and went for it."

"Knocked me right outta my bunk."

"Sorry," she apologized nice enough to make us square. She'd pulled me outta the soup a time or three over the years.

I shrugged, "No man while crossing the Up'n'up, so no real loss. But now we got us a predicament."

"How so?"

"I got no air and you got no fuel. And nothing short of the Phobos shipyard is gonna get these two girls apart."

She brought up an image of the *Lucy* and old *Elsie* from one of her tail-fin cameras. The forward third of the *Lucy* was buried right into the side of my craft.

"If ships ever had sex, these two gals are sure doing it." Jen had a way of making just about anything sound funny and we had a good chuckle together.

Over the second half of her bottle we set our minds to thinking some. Jen had knocked me off my course something fierce, what with applying a whole lotta sideways thrust vector, and it was going to take some doing to get us back. Even if a tug could get out this far, the *Lucy's* long range radio was buried inside the *Elsie's* hull. And the *Elsie's* antennas had once been right about where the *Lucy* had set her sights on my girl.

Adding to that, Jen's O2 needle was just fine for one gal out conquering the cosmos, but two of us was gonna be a strain that we was gonna have to do something about.

Took me a glance or two to figure out that I didn't like what I was seeing a' tall. One week, three days, three hours, three minutes—1:3:3:3 and counting the wrong direction once again.

So, no floating along 'til Earth Comm could be bothered to send a rescue.

We'd never heard of anyone else in this situation, but it did get us reminiscin' about some of the other snarls our classmates had gone and gotten theyselves tangled up in.

We talked about maybe piping some O2 over to my ship.

"Remember Clyde and how they found him?"

He'd gotten drunk as a skunk and run out of beer. They found him with keg tap and a welding torch about to cut into an O2 tank. "I thought it looked like a keg."

"Too bad, would have been one grand spectacle of a lightshow if he'd blowed himself up."

"He did," Jen reminded me. "Landed on Io and plonked right into one of the old volcanoes with a load of magnesium oxide aboard and that lava became a big old magnesium flow. Thermite burn-off was spectacular, brighter than Jupiter through the LaunchPub's dome on Europa where I'd been drinking some."

"Poor old Clyde never was the sharpest tack."

As we talked about other stories and tall tales, I got to thinkin' of my old Pap. Even now he'd be out at his favorite fishing stream, jug a moonshine at his side, just watching the ripples go by.

"Fish hides in the eddies," he'd say. "They duck in for a nap all the time, lazy cusses."

Now I was never gonna point out that his 'shine business could a-been much better if he had ambition—like his daughter what had qualified for space and all—and spent more time 'shining than fishing. But it was just the sort a man Pap was and I wasn't gonna gainsay him none. He'd been 'shinin' since his Pap had taught him and he'd earned his time just settin' down by the stream.

But it got me thinkin' about eddy currents and lazy circles. The beer and the whisky was catchin' up to me and I could almost feel myself goin' into a slow spin like them fishes.

"Hey!" We was down to one week, two days, and some...still counting the wrong direction.

"What?" Jen looked at me strange. She'd been smack in the middle of one of her best stories. I knew it well and always enjoyed the retelling. It was 'bout Missy Lou and the crazy Russian Vlad and how they thought they was being so sneaky, but Jen had reversed their cameras so the whole class had gotten into watching how little they knew about sex in zero-gee. It's a right awkward business with no gravity that takes some thought and a whole lot of practicing. Jen had provided a whole narrative to that there broadcast, then sent it off far and purty wide, just like Missy Lou's behind.

"I got me an idea."

Jen broke out a fresh bottle to celebrate, see why I like her, and I started telling her about fishin' holes and eddies and things that are mated up in space aside from big-bottomed girls and clumsy Russians.

It took us nigh on a week to get the rig worked up. That old clock was reading more like two days and heading fast for one before we got her finished.

The ships was all jammed up together cozy, but we figured we'd better run some welds to make sure. Being constructor ship gals, we scavenged the bent titanium frames and did some fast interior bracing work just to be all cautious-like.

It took a bit of figuring to crosswire the *Elsie's* engine controls to the *Lucy's* console, but with the help of a keg or two that I floated over, I got her done.

We sobered up 'nuf to take some good sightings, then I fired off the *Elsie's* engines just as the clock ticked over to 0:0:23:59—one day to get us into Mars or we were gonna be two very unhappy gals.

I could only do a little burst. With the *Lucy*

still all buried deep inside her, my girl's center-of-load was way off center and in moments we was spinning just like that old eddy current.

Each time the *Elsie's* engines was lined up all right, I gave her another bit of a nudge. We was soon getting kinda pinned to one side of the cockpit by that there spinning we were doing.

"We're headed in the right direction," Jen read off some of the instruments, "but I'm gonna be a dizzy bitch by the time we get there."

"Always were, Jen." My body was the type that needed a man who wanted to do a whole lot of handling. Jen's was more the type that let her handle any man she wanted and brother did she.

One of the things I'd always liked best 'bout havin' Jen along was her general cheerfulness. Another thing was she always drew a lot of the male kind of attention, but as there was only one of her, there was always some fine pickings left off on the side. She was always glad to share. Being a gal above Terra's atmo made us a rare commodity in the second place, but in the first, Jen had a whole powerful gravity well all her own that was right fun to be close to.

But she did have a point.

With each pop of the old engines we was spinning less like a lazy eddy current with one a Pap's fishing hidin' in her and more like the water at the bottom of the toilet bowl.

I'd set the engine to auto-fire at the right point of each spin, and soon it was just easier to lie on the side hull and giggle together over girl talk.

"Remember, old Ralphie?" (Tole you earlier I *was gonna get to Ralphie in a bit.)*

"Now that was a major loss," Jen agreed. Ralphie had made a study of them Old Indian ways, even though there wasn't no more India, of how to go about makin' a girl especially happy. Both me and Jen had reason to know he was real good at it. Then the boy had met a Brazilian girl what had done the same with stuff she'd learnt from some old Incas. He'd gone back to being a grounder and stopped sharing his skills with his old space pals. It was a sad thing indeed.

"Wasn't one bit fair of him to switch like that," Jen was gettin' some heat up as we lay side by side against the hull and considered the situation. "What self-respecting woman takes a good man off the market anyways? That kinda flip-flop just ain't right."

And while Jen had a point, I was thinking a flip-flop was just what we needed. Because if this spin kept building much longer, I wouldn't be able to reach up to my keg, which I'd strapped right close to the copilot's chair.

I clawed my way back up the old spin-force well. Jen wasn't in much condition to follow, but I made it with her helpful shove or two against my behind.

I timed a hard hit with the attitude jets and got the two ships flipped over the other way. Now with each burst of the big engines our spin slowed some. I refilled another beer and hung on until Jen floated free and was headed my way. Then, with more spins and engine firings, we was driftin' to the other side of the cabin.

"Dang, I forgot to take the keg with me."

"Just as well," Jen pointed out. "Need some reason to crawl back up to the controls for the next flip."

With each engine burst we'd been picking up speed nice as could be toward Phobos.

It wasn't 'til the fourth or maybe fifth time

we did the flip and I hit the keg in passing that I had another itch to think about than the one I was hoping some boy would be scratchin' when we hit the Low-Gee down on the red planet. Maybe after a short stop for a little celebrating at the No-Gee on Phobos—which weren't quite true as Jen weighed two ounces here and I weighed more'n three—but we wouldn't argue about it's name none as long as we got to stand there in one piece.

"Jen."

"Uh-huh?"

"We done a good job of picking up some speed here."

"High-five, girl," she held up a palm and I slapped it some. Had to stare into my beer bulb a moment to remember what I'd thought up.

"Phobos. It's coming up right quick."

"Yes!" Jen pumped a fist. "Men await!"

"We done forgot something though."

"Doesn't matter. Men await!" See why I like Jen? She keeps a sharp eye, or even a bleary one on what important is going on.

"Jen, we ain't got the time or the room to slow back down enough." That old arrival clock was down around six hours and we'd took eighteen to get to where we were. Worse, I'd bet my suit was empty again from all of the cargo bay welding we'd been doing.

"No men?" She sounded right pitiful, a girl denied her favorite toy, and I hated to do that to her. Or to me, what with the old itch itching and all.

"Maybe I have an idea though."

"Good! Bring her on."

"How do you feel about aero-braking?"

"In Martian atmo? I dunno," her brow furrowed up some. "Mighty thin stuff. They don't even have enough to breathe."

"Figured that. But if we swung close enough, we could get some grab."

"Men. Grab men! Yes!" Jen pumped a fist again, then looked over at me careful-like. "How close?"

I did some serious thinking about Mars' atmo, 'bout two beers worth. "Real close." Heat of passage was gonna scorch the soil. Just might bump into an old rover or two if we wasn't careful.

"Huh," Jen went quiet for a while. "Well, not something I'd want to try sober."

"Nope!" Tole ya' Jen was smart.

With a shared nod, we dragged ourselves back to the keg. I thumped the can with my foot and we still had plenty.

Once we got her dialed in, I looked at the console. I decided that I was not happy with what I saw there and drew another brew as fast as she'd go.

Sober or not, I finally knew that the Old Maker Man had him one nasty sense of humor.

The nav clock was reading out our time to Martian atmo: 13:33. 13:32…

Intro to: The Gals Team

I decided to make this my last story. A whole lot things changed out here, I'll be careful-like not to give things away much afore I get to the story though.

By the time this story come along, me and the *Elsie* had been cruisin' the Up'n'up over a decade. I'd even sold some of these here tales which surprised me no end. I thought about sending copies to my Pap, but he weren't exactly what you'd call a lettered man, not like me, so I decided not to bother him none.

Me and Jen had been best gal friends just as long. Never held it against her none for when she ran the *Lucy* into the side of my old *Elsie.* That's what best gal friends do for each other. They help out.

The Up'n'up ain't what it used to be neither. Was a time when a gal could be the first soul to step somewhere, setting up stations for them science types afore they ever showed up and such. They was "the explorers," never mentioned us much. Now, people is most everywhere. I done heard that Tycho had put in an actual pool for swimming, with a slide and all.

Don't that beat all.

Not bein' much of a bikini-type gal, I ain't gone to see it yet. Jen did though. She is a serious bikini-type gal, what with coming from Hawaii before the volcano made sure there was no more Hawaii. Almost went with her just to see for myself how much of a bikini-type gal she was.

"Nothing but a lot of ground-pounders," she complained in the Tycho Tavern after. "Can you believe they let tourists into the Up'n'up. That just isn't right."

Now ol' Dean who ran the Tycho didn't let none of that type into his pub and we an' the other drivers and Loonies was right thankful to him and gave him lots of patronage and a fair chunk of our wages.

But things is still changin' fast out here. Them Olympic Games is gonna be on two planets and Luna. Earth and Mars, of course. The committee said that the time lag to Europa was too long, 'special as it weren't in conjunction with the others none at the right time.

That upset the up-system folk more'n any Hatfields and McCoys. They're holdin' their own games at the same time. Well, almost. Me and Jen mighta helped 'em some to set up a big old set of transmitters. Up-system will be having their games ahead of the inner-folk, but with just enough time lag so that their broadcasting will blast down on the inner planets like a revenooer and his hounds yapping 'til a 'shiner can't hear hisself think right at the same moment as them inner-system events.

Mercury is holding out against being Solar Stupid. Got banners what says that and all which makes me kinda proud that folks like my stories.

I heard something funny 'bout them mass

drivers…they keep breaking. My old friend down there near the sun is still brewin' the beer. She's gettin' good at it, so I always try to check in on her when I run a load down her way. She still gives the best kinda send-off a gal could ever want. Her greetin's are mighty good too. Maybe I shouldn'ta tole her how to reprogram the B4 Buss inside them robots heads…or maybe I shoulda. Everything gets real peaceful on that old rock each time them robots throw theyselves into the mass drivers and blow theyselves up.

Anyways, here's my last story about me and the *Elsie*. And my best friend Jen, of course.

THE GALS TEAM

"*That's not exactly a* pretty sight."

I hated to see my best friend Jen looking all sad, but it was hard to argue. We'd gotten our ships into Phobos shipyard, but even the tugs were having trouble with 'em. When you run a Class Three hull into the side of a Class Four faster than a revenooer man chasing a 'shiner, the results is never good. Then the welding them together hadn't helped the look of things so much.

"Nice color black on the hull, though."

That's why I like Jen, she could always find a bright side. We'd scorched them hulls right good doing our aero-braking to slow down while goin' around Mars. Though the sonic boom we'd made over the new construction in the deeps of Valles Marineris canyon hadn't been appreciated none. We'd ducked down there 'cause the air was extra thick and helped us slow some extra.

But I wanted to join in with Jen on being positive and all.

"And we're alive."

"We are." She said it in a surprised sorta way.

"Which means we get more chances at finding us some good men."

"Yes!" That cheered her up the rest of the way.

"Sure made a mess of those ships," the yard manager came over just to take the happy glow off the day. Some people was just like that.

I was considering telling him a thing or three about what my Pap would say about people like him when Jen stopped me.

"What is that?"

Me and Mr. Gloom turned to look at where her blue eyes was aimed.

Now it weren't no Class Five hull. That was

'bout the shortest lived class of ships in the history of ever.

The first Class Five exploded on ignition an' took out a fair chunk of a space station. Scattered bits of itself all over a place called Poughkeepsie like anyone who didn't live there might care. Barely made the news up here.

Second one got to old Luna just fine, but didn't think much of stopping and made a nice new crater right where one of them Apollo museums was. Didn't matter much. There were like a half dozen of the things and nobody ever went to visit more than one—once bein' plenty to see that them pioneers was eight kinds of crazy.

The third and last Class Five nobody would get on. So they put in some new-fangled robot autopilot. She immediately turned tail and ran. She was last seen headin' into the old Kuiper Belt past Neptune with her engine still firing hard. Whether it was the robot or the ship what was doin' it, neither of them was tellin' us and them Class Fives was done with.

Now what Jen had spotted were like a Class Four. My *Elsie* were a Class Four and she were as reliable as a rock—exceptin' up here in the

Up'n'up where rocks had a way of surprisin' a gal when she least wanted to be surprised. *Elsie* didn't do that none.

But what Jen was lookin' at also *weren't* like a Class Four. She was near enough twice the size an' had her six engines 'stead a two.

"It's the new Class Six," Mr. Gloom had perked up some.

That set me and Jen to laughin' mighty hard.

"Not a space jock with an ounce of common sense who would set foot in such a thing," Jen went into a fit of merry giggles that was cute as could be on her.

Mr. Gloom looked mighty put out. "She's got the Class Four control system. So we know that's good. Same engines too, just four more of them. She's safe, fast, and more powerful than anything else in the system."

Now that sobered us some and got me to thinking. Thinkin' and lookin' back over my shoulder at the sad mess of the *Elsie* and the *Lucy* all scrunched together. Don't get me wrong, I love my *Elsie,* but she did look mighty tired compared to that pretty new Class Six.

"Gal could get from pub to pub mighty

fast in one of those," Jen was thinkin' along the same way I was thinkin'.

It's the kinda thing that best friends does.

"What's she cost?" Jen was always the practical gal.

"It's free," Mr. Gloom was also Mr. Dumb. Weren't no way that shiny piece of ship were free.

Pap done taught me that lesson good: "Ain't no such thing as free, not even a lunch. Hell, ain't hardly no bargains no more neither. Says 'free' they still gonna get you in the fine print." And while Pap weren't much of a fine-print man, I got the idea right clear.

"What's the fine print?" I asked Mr. Gloom.

"Where the hell you gals been that you ain't heard?" And he handed us a flyer afore walking away like it was us something was wrong with.

We looked it over together.

Win a Class Six ship!
Grand Prize of new reality show:
That Ship's Mine!
Competition will run throughout
known space.

Finals to be held live from the Low-Gee Lounge on Mars!

And it went on and on promising all sorts of fine things. When we tapped the display on the spec sheet, well, that got Jen's and my attention right quick. A Class Six weren't just a big Class Four, she were a thing of beauty right down to three-tenths-gee acceleration—triple what the old *Elsie* could do and four times the *Lucy*.

That flyer said the competition was startin' right soon. We skipped the Phobos No-Gee, excepting for a couple of beers and to make sure that Mr. Gloom wasn't having us on. He weren't. It was all anyone was talkin' 'bout.

Down to the Low-Gee, the old place was hopping.

"Gonna have to import some kegs if this keeps up," Dean told us with a smile and a wink as he slipped across a pair of pitchers for us. Kept meaning to ask him if he was any relation to Tycho Tavern Dean, but kept forgettin' and now he were too busy.

The Low-Gee too was buzzing with all the hot competition news. Seems as holders of actual Up'n'up pilot cards we weren't in the first rounds. 'Stead of just making it among us fliers, they'd started with all the amateurs.

"Kinda makes sense," I told Jen. "Way more a them than us."

All kindsa folks was in and even being our charming selfs we didn't get our favorite booth. So we scooted a couple of Martian ground-pounder gal types out of another one what weren't too bad and sat back to watch the show. The Low-Gee had a big old vidwall above the bar. I 'member back in the early days when it was covered with posters of tri-D movie stars wearing little or nothin'. It had been all women posters back then, 'til me and Jen started putting up some nice male ones right alongside. Them men in the Low-Gee Lounge learned right quick not to argue none with Jen—and them posters stayed.

'Bout five years back it was the Low-Gee got her first vidwall, but this one was new and she was a monster. And instead the usual show of men and women havin' adventures and getting all kinds a cozy before, after, and even during them adventures, it was all space and flyin' rigs.

Took us a bit to sort out that it was the "Big Game." Was Jen what noticed the score counters all down one side. Thirty-four days it had been running. Thousands a ground-pounders was working their way up.

"I still don't understand," Jen kept pouring while she was wondering, so I listened along, "how they can give away an entire ship as a prize?"

It was Pap's comment 'bout fine print what had me thinking on it. Then I spotted the how. Right there acrost the bottom a the screen was running a whole mess of ads for things what no normal person needs. Maybe Jen, being from a big city and all, didn't notice them ads, but they sure stood out to this country gal.

There was more up the sides, 'crost the top, and all over the place. Even the ships that were flying in the game kept flashing racy little logos.

Then I started into looking at the main part a the screen. It was a giant simulator all cluttered up with ships and planets and things.

There was flyin' challenges like obstacle courses. And landing challenges and all the sorts of stuff a gal drivin' the Up'n'up gotta do with her days. Some of them ground-pounders was purty funny, runnin' head on inta space stations and things, but some of 'em weren't half bad.

I watched through a couple three beers and considered. The game made flyin' look just as fine as it sometimes was.

"Not a one of 'em I'd trust with a load of Pap's 'shine," I tole Jen. Though I have to admit all quiet-like that there was some challenges I wouldn't be too happy 'bout trying myself, if they was real. This thing got tougher by the hour while we watched it.

Though if that display was telling the truth, them Class Sixes was downright amazing ships. Wasn't a flyer in the Up'n'up wouldn't want one for hisself.

"I need that ship," Jen turned to me. Yep! They even got old Jen's attention.

"For what?" I was starting to lose interest in that big ol' game. After all, me and Jen had just come back from a passel of time in space. On top of that, what with nearly dyin' and all, I was ready for a little distraction, the kind menfolk was good at givin'. We never had no vids when I was sprouting up back in them marshes with Pap. Pap were strictly an old-school kinda person and I was his daughter. That game were just some game.

"For flying," Jen was being persistent-like. And she weren't doing that crookin' her pinkie at menfolk that she did so well. You could see the disappointment on the faces of the mens what were nearby.

Reluctant-like, I turned back to look up at that big ol' screen.

"See?" She pointed of to a part of the scorebox I hadn't noticed so much. "The Up'n'up fliers start tomorrow. Let's sign up."

"I got me the *Elsie*. Don't need no Six." But I was watchin' out of the corner of eye kinda. I seed one of them ships doing a Jupiter aerobrake just as clean as a knife. If a ground-pounder could do it, made me wonder what I could do with her.

I gave a kinda shrug, what with Jen being so eager and all.

She'd hung onto that old flyer Mr. Gloom had given us back to Phobos. She had it out and tapped the application.

"Uh-oh."

Now Jen and I go back a long ways.

Sometimes when she says "Uh-oh" it's all funny 'cause she's about to trip a man or three and fall into their laps. Sometimes it's just a I-need-a-fresh-pitcher-of-beer-real-soon "Uh-oh." But then every once in a while it's more in the think-quick-or-we're-gonna-die kinda category. This time it was kinda in that last category so I decided to pay some serious attention.

"What?" I finally got around to askin'. Maybe I needed some food before I dug too much deeper into my second pitcher.

"Entry fee. A big one."

I looked down at where Jen was lookin' and decided that I should skip that food and just keep workin' on the beer. It was a number bigger'n a bar tab, which was a pretty substantial number at times.

But then I did some lookin' to the fine print just like Pap taught me.

"Lookee who be in charge of approving them applications."

Jen looked, then she turned to me and smiled one of her big happy smiles. We finished our pitchers and went hunting.

Cash and Ty had done right good for

theyselves. They wasn't just Johnny Law on Tycho no more, trying to harass a new flyer what had melted their pretty gantry a little bit. They was now head of Johnny Laws for all Mars. Once we tracked 'em down we set right into renewing old times for old times' sake. Weren't too far into the next morning when Jen slipped the old applications out and Cash and Ty marked 'em paid in full.

Now the judgin' part wasn't going to be so easy, nor half so fun. Whole system was watchin' now. They'd gotten hooked on the ads and competition and such and couldn't look away now. That part deep inside that always dreamed of goin' into space had hooked everybody. Betsy and Nancy told me—seein' as how we'd stayed in touch some so that I could know Pap was okay—that even Jake had tried. Course he wasn't as careful as Pap and was doin' some time for gettin' caught with his cattle sellin' business, but he'd done applied from inside the pen anyway. Never thought Jake had them kinda dreams inside him.

The first couple days that we real spacer types was playin' changed things a whole bunch. There's tricks you learn in the Up'n'up that the simulator knew just what to do with. They set up a dozen a them machines in the Low-Gee and let us go agin them ground-pounders however we wish't. Soon there was just a couple Earthers left.

Then there was a long break while all the finalists was flown up to the Low-Gee in brand new Class Sixes. It was quite the spectacle and you jes' knew that PE, Ore Transport, and all them others was going to be changing out their hulls soon as could be. Folks what built the Sixes musta had a sharp girl in advertising, 'cause giving away the first one was gonna be a bargain for her bossfolks.

Me and Jen was sittin' in the Low-Gee the night before the grand finale—got our favorite booth back purty easy by that point, as we stayed high in them standings.

Every flyer up and down the system was parked in the Low-Gee, but a whole mess of 'em hadn't done so good. We was among the conquering heroes and a whole lot of the other pilots was bein' real nice about cheerin' us gals on. Them men had certainly done 'nuff cheering me up the last couple nights that there weren't no way to be sad a'tall.

"Did you know there was so many flyin' the Up'n'up?" I asked Jen quiet-like.

She just shook her head in a shower of blond hair that got so many menfolks's attention it took us some doin' to wave them off. We was havin' a jaw 'bout things more important than men. Didn't happen often, but this was one a them times.

"Don't know how you're gonna win this, Jen," I wanted her to be let down gentle if she didn't. She was a heck of a pilot, but we wasn't the only ones what had been walkin' the Up'n'up for so long.

"Most of the fliers are out already. They're just waiting to see the bloodbath." Jen pointed up to the vidwall.

There was long list of names in faded gray. Miccin, Two Dog, Emmet…there was a whole buncha good fliers what wasn't gonna be flying their own Class Six notime soon.

"Vaco and Tiny Tex are still in." Vaco really was crazy and I was sure that Tiny Tex was still tiny, but I wasn't going to waste any time checkin' that out.

But I thought about them some. Pap was the best 'shiner there ever was, but other than that one time he opened up about Ma saying as how she was a dreamin'-type gal like me, I never seed him take no interest in a woman.

"Maybe," I changed over to doin' my thinkin' out loud, "'cause they ain't so interesting to us women folk, all they got for theyselves is the flyin'."

"Makes sense," Jen agreed.

"Evgenia's out," I noticed. Could never tell if she were interested in men, women, nor nobody 'ceptin' herself. Never was sure what to think 'bout her.

"Good," Jen said it kinda fierce, but I knew she didn't mean no harm by it. Wasn't a nasty bone anywhere in Jen's curvy body.

"We're both still in." Hadn't been all that hard what with the practice I'd had getting outta scrapes.

"But you're right," Jen got serious all of sudden. "You're a better pilot than I am. To win we're going to need something better than piloting."

Such a thing coming from my best friend Jen set me back hard. It was like when Pap tole me I done good patchin' his still. Made me feel kinda sniffly and I had to quaff down some beer right quick to keep my throat from getting all tight.

"Maybe," I tole Jen, "it was from all the practice Pap gave me when we was runnin' shine. He'd sit in the passenger seat, with his favorite jug held tight, and tell me where to go. Got so good, he could sometimes nod off and I'd do just fine. Johnny Law never caught me. Well, the deputy did once, but I paid him off real pleasant and quiet-like in the tall grass. Pap slept right through and never knew."

"That's it! Come on!" And Jen was up and out of our booth afore we'd even finished the first pitcher.

While I hate leavin' any perfectly good beer behind unfinished, I recalled how Jen had never led me astray. Not even that first time back in Tycho. So I followed her through all them disappointed men and out to the room we was sharin'.

She went digging through the pile a clothes that always appeared all magical-like wherever Jen was. I swear that woman couldn't even set down a sealed pack without a flurry of clothes just a poppin' out in all directions.

"Try this on."

"Jen, you know your clothes won't fit me none. I'm a big gal case you done fergit."

"Just trust me. Strip down and try this on." It was one of Jen's big nightshirts. She only wore 'em when she wanted to make a man extra-happy when he gets to take it back off her. I always been more of a nightgown gal.

I took off what I was wearing and Jen let out one of them low, saucy whistles.

"Damn, girl."

I looked where she was lookin' then looked back up from my big melons to her. "It's just me. Don't see what big deal I is that you be whistlin' like that."

"I just haven't ever seen you naked. No wonder the menfolk go so crazy when you're around."

"Me? It's you what does that to them."

"Nope. Oh, I have fun and all, but they barely take notice of me when you're around."

I had to laugh at that. A manfolk not paying attention to a bundle as cute as Jen just didn't make no sense. She gave over her nightshirt and I tugged and tucked and squirmed 'til I had her on. It was a tight fit, but I made it in.

"Now we're talking!" Jen nodded somethin' fierce as she surveyed me up and down.

I turned for a mirror to see what in heck she was talkin' 'bout. Maybe she'd gotten into some of Pap's 'shine. Though maybe not. My old melons was pretty darned impressive what with spending their last ten years in low- and no-gee kinda places.

Jen moved up beside me and began pushing things about, shiftin' and nudgin' 'til she was happy with how they sat in that stretched-tight nightshirt of hers. There was something that about how she handled them big breasts that no man ever understood. A gal just knew how they was connected to your body. Tuggin' and grabbin' and pullin' just ain't all that much fun from the women's side. But Jen knew that and handled mine in ways that had me thinkin' some very nice thoughts.

"There," she declared.

I looked in the mirror and knew she was right. If I was man I'd be lookin' at my chest plenty too.

"Any pilot worth his salt is gonna take one good look at you tomorrow and he's never gonna think right again. Because, damn girl, that is one fine look on you." She turned me sideways in the mirror and did some more of that nice adjustin' she'd been doing. Maybe she had a point.

"Now what about you?"

"Me?" Jen said. "I'll just do my usual."

I knowed what her "usual" looked like. Somethin' thin and clingy-like that tole men exactly what they'd be gettin' if they could get it off her. Then I got to thinkin' of Betsy back to home, always fallin' out of her dress. Jen already had the landin' on her back part of it down.

I dug down deep in my pack until I found the bit of filmy that had been a present las' time I was down-system to Mercury. It was a bright red sweater what the bartender down there had knit up just like hers, but in my size. Except she made it kinda lacy-like, so there was little bits of skin showin' every which way.

"Strip down and try this on," I held it out to Jen just the way she'd done to me.

She looked at me just as funny as I musta looked at her, but she did what I tole her. No matter what Jen says, she is one put together gal and I'll admit to doin' a little admirin' myself along the way of her changing things.

"This is ridiculous," Jen argued from somewhere deep inside that sweater as she tangled with it.

I give her a hand, tuggin' here and there. Then slipping out a big handful or two of that soft gold hair of hers that always looked so nice and getting it settled on her shoulders.

First thing that sweater did was fall off one of her shoulders and slide down far enough that you could see a fair part of her womanness.

Jen tugged the shoulder back into place and the other one let go. She went to do it again and I set my hands on her shoulders and stood her in front a me facin' that mirror.

"Watch," I tole her. Then I tugged up the fallen shoulder and t'other fell and slipped even lower than afore. She got a fine collarbone and long neck. Mix in the bare shoulder plus that nice galish-shaped bit, an' she looked like one of them models in the vids just invitin' you to come and take it all off'n her. That sweater was big enough on her that maybe by just pullin' in both shoulders at once, it might fall right off'n her.

Jen tugged at a shoulder once or twice more, then smiled up at me in the mirror.

Now Jen's smile is a right powerful weapon that I seen her deploy against poor unsuspectin' men more'n once. And it never failed on them. Must say, could kinda feel it workin' on me too.

I looked at us some more in the mirror. We was two purty powerful women and we looked even better'n than we did most days.

Now I ain't no smart gal like my best friend Jen, but I ain't no boondocks gal no more neither. I been places and I've seed things.

And one of the nicest things I'd seed in a long while was Jen shruggin' that sweater off both her shoulders at once and it just slidin' down onto the floor. That and her big smile as I grabbed a holt of her from behind right there in the mirror.

That next day, we proved that most men just wasn't up to our superior woman-type planning. They was walkin' into walls and hatchways while watchin' us loose-hipped and happy gal-type friends walk into that competition together. Half the remaining field never even made it through the first obstacle in the simulator, an' it weren't a hard one. There was crashes and klaxons galore louder than a whole flock of revenooer men hot on the scent of a whole fleet of stills.

After that it helped some that the field was small enough now that they was putting the pilots' pictures up next to our ships in the display as we flew. Most of the boys it was just a little picture of their heads and not much more, so as the audience could see their expressions and other thinkin' they was doin' as they flew. Us two women-folk, they aimed them cameras in other places. As more 'n' more was knocked outta the game, the pilots' pictures was made bigger 'n' bigger. Us gals in particular.

But by lunchtime, when me and Jen was strategizin' over a few beers, we knew there was still trouble ahead.

"It's not enough," Jen harrumphed in frustration. "Crazy Vaco is still in. Those two Earther boys must have been born with a game paddle in their hands, and then there's a couple of old hands who are just like us—good old boys who've seen it all and are good fliers besides."

Now Jen was awful heated up 'bout winnin' that ship and all and I hated to disappoint her. So I set into thinkin' of things I might know that could help us out some. Thought about some of the scrapes we'd been in and out of over the years and the stories we told about them. I thought about some of the good times too. Though that turned out to be a dangerous place to be thinkin'—'cause rememberin' last night and how good it had been 'tween me and Jen kinda made the time slide by real easy-like and there weren't a whole lot of that left.

Then I got me to thinkin' about Pap. Pap was always a real practical sort and he weren't no fan of losing neither. Not a dime on a jug nor a drop to Johnny Law.

Now Pap had done good for hisself and he'd provided for me even when I was no more than another mouth to feed. But Nancy and Sue done told me how Pap was fishin' more and 'shining less since I been gone. Now Pap has as much right to his leisure years as any hard-working city man, but maybe it was more'n that. Together we'd made one formidable-type 'shining team.

That had me looking about the Low-Gee.

Most of them menfolk what was still in the competition was sittin' all separate at different tables. They had their buddies about 'em, but they was busy eyeing each other. Eyein' us too, and not just for how nice our clothes was fitting. Even the old hands, though they sat at the same table, wasn't talkin' to each other. Not like me and Jen.

Not like me and Jen.

We was different.

We was womenfolk.

Them men was all workin' on how to get the best of their buddies. I was tryin' to figure how to get Jen the Class Six ship she was wantin' so bad.

"Hey Jen."

"Uh-huh," she was staring down into her beer and was so hunched that she was on the verge of losin' my sweater off her whole body again. I tugged up one side to cover her nice shoulder so it'd stay for now. I had me an idea and didn't want no distractin' from my thinkin'.

"Ever tell you 'bout my old Pap and them revenooer hounds?"

She squinted up at me, "I don't think so."

"Well, hounds is a real problem. Once they

got the scent of you or your still, takes a whole lot to make 'em let go of it."

"So what do you do?"

"Some folks spread about steaks with rat poison in it. But Pap don't hold truck with that. 'Not the poor critters' fault they was brought up on the wrong side of the law.' Pap always was partial to hounds."

"How did your Pap handle them?"

"Rabbits. He'd place 'em all around with a bit a rotten string a holding them in place. He'd set 'em there in the marsh, on their string, with a nice piece of lettuce. They'd sit there eatin' just as happy as could be. Right up 'til a hound come along."

Jen always did like my stories and she perked right up. "Let me guess. When the hounds came, the rabbits would jump hard enough to break the string and bolt into the woods."

"And the hounds would run after 'em pretty as you could please."

"And it worked?"

"Sure," then I shrugged 'cause that weren't the whole truth. "It worked 'ceptin' the time the rabbit run straight to Pap's still and tried hiding under it."

Jen's big laugh came out for a stroll about the room and I could see all of the menfolk looking at us with some serious worryin' going on.

"So, I was thinkin' what if I run rabbit? I can be distractin' them men, leading 'em into places they don't wanna be or cain't get out from. Then you go ahead and win the ship pretty as you please."

Jen was nodding happily.

Minded me of how she looked as I took her down in front of that mirror last night.

"I've got an even better idea."

As Jen was the smart one, I set in to listenin'.

"You're the better pilot. I'm better at teasing men. I'll do the rabbiting; you win the ship."

"But then it won't be your ship," I hated pointing out the error in Jen's high-brow thinkin', but it was there, so like the best friend I was, I done it anyways.

Then she pulled out that flyer she'd been hangin' onto about this old competition and showed me something I hadn't noticed before. Then we was sharing smiles and laughs much to the upset of all them others crowded into the Low-Gee Lounge.

Well, that's just how I won that Class Six hull.

Jen ran rabbit, leadin' them men all over simulated space and back. And I quietly slid across the finish first and with the most points.

I got me all kinds of awards and praise for bein' the "Best Gal Pilot in the Up'n'up." I'd a-pointed out I was the best pilot, not just the best *gal* pilot, but Pap had never liked it much when I spoke out of turn, so I kept my mouth shut.

Jen had some other ideas what with being raised so smart and all. She said more'n a few words 'bout that, shoulda knowed she would.

It was Jen bein' so smart that had her noticin' something in the old contest flyer what none of them men had. Or mayhaps they did, but didn't care. The Class Six she's rated for two pilots, not one. Men would just hire some grounder they could lord everything over.

Not me and Jen.

When I won the ship, we both got a berth. We was a team when we won and we still is.

I did get to name that ol' Class Six, which was right nice of Jen to let me do. We call her the *Elsie II* and at times it feels just like Ma is flying with us. We still enjoy trippin' menfolk when we're in port. But out in the great dark of the Up'n'up, there's a whole lot of time when it's just me and Jen.

That reminds me. Got one other thing along with the ship and compliments and awards and all.

They also give me a real fine jacket. Genuine red leather with my name stitched right 'cross one breast and a big ol' image of the *Elsie II* 'cross the back. Some-a the times it's all Jen wears for whole weeks aboard ship. Must say I like that a fair bit. It just slips off'n her shoulders in the nicest way.

Wrappin' It Up Some

That's why this is the last story of me and *Elsie*. She done her journey and never did leave that old scrap yard on Phobos. But me and Jen and the *Elsie II,* we ever since been burning across the Up'n'up from Mercury Station—where me and Jen both get very fine greetin's whenever we drop in—on out to the Kuiper Belt.

It's like the old days out there. Folks just drinkin' and humpin' and gettin' it done the way it's supposed to be done, or near 'nuff as no never mind to them what stays down-system.

I'd like to leave you with a piece a Pap's wisdom, but all that comes to mind is the last

words he ever done said to me. We was standin'
at that bus station where he dropped me off
to go to the Up'n'up. He'd gived me my goin'
away present of a whole case of his finest and
we was both lookin' down at it tryin' to find
words to say.

Course it were Pap what found them words
first 'cause he was always so wise:

"Give 'em hell, girl."

Done my best, Pap. I done my best.

About the Author

M. L. Buchman has over 50 novels and 30 short stories in print. His military romantic suspense books have been named Barnes & Noble and NPR "Top 5 of the year" and twice *Booklist* "Top 10 of the Year," placing two titles on their "Top 101 Romances of the Last 10 Years" list. He has been nominated for the Reviewer's Choice Award for "Top 10 Romantic Suspense of the Year" by *RT Book Reviews* and was a 2016 RWA RITA finalist. In addition to romance, he also writes thrillers, fantasy, and science fiction.

In among his career as a corporate project

manager he has: rebuilt and single-handed a fifty-foot sailboat, both flown and jumped out of airplanes, designed and built two houses, and bicycled solo around the world.

He is now making his living as a full-time writer on the Oregon Coast with his beloved wife. He is constantly amazed at what you can do with a degree in Geophysics. You may keep up with his writing by subscribing to his newsletter at www.mlbuchman.com.

If you enjoyed this story, you might also enjoy:

Night Rescue (excerpt)
-a Future Night Stalkers story-

"*Good morning, Takara.*"

"Good morning to you, *Stella,*" Captain Takara Olmsted, 160th Charlie Company, crossed the habitat's hangar floor and patted her Stinger on the nose before she started the pre-spaceflight inspection. Some pilots didn't

like their ships greeting them and switched off the functionality; spouting some tripe that they could write a more imaginative program while scratching their backsides. And for some of her fellow pilots, that was the most creative part of their anatomy.

Takara had always found it rather sweet—once she'd programmed out the factory's deep male voice that didn't fit her craft at all. The voice they'd shipped her with was a bad imitation of a passé interactives star. Or perhaps it really was Jess Brock fallen on hard times; an IA star's moments of glory were even shorter than all but the unluckiest soldier's. Not that she'd ever been a fan, not even a little. Didn't matter. Takara hadn't just changed the selection, she'd erased all the others out of the ship's banks once she'd found *Stella's* true voice.

A Stinger-60 Block III might be eighty meters of flying death to the enemy, but the *Stella* was a dainty girl in or out of atmo, quick on her thrusters and ready to dance. She was also chic, space black with a near non-existent profile on enemy scopes, could carry a platoon of SpecOps in full fieldsuits, and was armed to the frickin' teeth.

All were attributes that Takara did her best to emulate, except for the carrying-a-platoon thing. Even off base she dressed in black darker than her long straight fall of hair—cutting edge materials so light-absorbing that she was often told she looked like a hole in the space-time continuum. *Perfect!* She stayed sleek, fit, and was as skilled at hand-to-hand combat as she was at piloting during deep-space warfare.

The rest of her crew arrived together in the Colony's hangar, a tight metal box in the zero-G sector that was little bigger than her craft. They were a good team, sharp and dedicated. And it wasn't that they were late; they were early. But Takara had always been earlier. Even as a cadet she'd been first to class and first to the drill field.

"Still the sky-eater, Captain," her port-gunner greeted her the same way he always did.

"Still," the copilot answered before Takara could.

"Always will be," the starboard gunner agreed.

"And damned proud of it," Takara finished their pre-flight ritual.

They all laughed and made fast work of inspecting the *Stella*. She was immaculate; no service crews in the air corps like the 160th Night Stalkers. Takara tried to imagine the long-ago crazies who had taken to the night in fragile rotary craft, flying at night by nav gear little better than a torch and a compass. She shuddered, glad to be living in this time despite the troubles.

At the end of their inspection, she rubbed *Stella's* nose for good luck.

They were going to need it.

* * *

Intruder neutralization off.
Door open.
Recognize four boarding.
Seal and secure.
Input ready for mission profile.
Mission plan loaded.
Fuel = plan + 50%. Check.
Ammo = plan (0)[really?] + full charge COIL laser. Check.
Air = sufficient 4 crew 6 months or full load 1 week + regen. Check.
Plan was…Oh dear! Definitely not check.

* * *

Major Rick Coralto, commander of the 160th's Alpha Company, punched the fist of his combat suit against the center of *Jess'* entry door. "Hey, buddy."

"Hey, Rick," the outer airlock door pulled in two centimeters then slid aside.

It always cracked him up that his Stinger sounded just like Rick's favorite IA hero when Rick had been going through flight school. Jess Brock, Secret Agent—sappy as hell, but Jess always won, always had the best toys, and always got the hottest women. Not that Rick was complaining; unlike Jess' toys, Rick's Stinger was real. But the voice was so good that sometimes Rick wondered if Jess Brock was hiding somewhere aboard. It was just that laid back. The "I'm in perfect control of the situation" tone just slayed him.

Rick maneuvered his combat suit into the crew's airlock, stepped it back into the charging cradle and waited for the rest of his crew to float in behind him.

Rick's crew and the rest of 160th Night Stalkers Alpha Company were just finishing a training mission with the Brits out at the L2 Lagrange Point, sixty-thousand klicks beyond the Lunar Farside.

Good location choice to set up a nation, Rick had acknowledged. The massive O'Neill Colony habitat could hold a couple million citizens apiece. And L2 was the one place where no direct line of fire existed from the Earth. It was definitely a tactical sweet spot that he wished his people had grabbed first.

Last night, after the mock battles had been won (by the Night Stalkers of course), they'd been invited ashore for a big meal and a little bit of drinking that had turned into a lot of drinking and a little bit of meal…and almost a very cute British Leftenant, but that hadn't worked out in the end. He still wasn't sure why, he'd had on his Jess Brock blue-and-gold jumpsuit and been at his most charming. Maybe if he'd spotted her before he drank several of the Brits under the table.

He was feeling clearheaded, considering, but was glad that the SCS—Stinger Command System—knew more about flying than he'd ever be able to learn. Though control of the ships hadn't been given to the computers since the International Law of Control had passed, they still had all of their computers intact. And on the SCS, that was a lot of computer.

He and his crew slid into their seats with a collective groan, they'd all enjoyed themselves last night. Then they began powering up the various systems; Rick thumbing in to convince the software that a human pilot was aboard.

The I-LoC had been one of the last things that the nations of the solar system had agreed on. Now even lowly cargo ships always had human pilots. Law of Control had meant there were a lot of idiots in space, but it had finally ended the Drone Downfall that had almost erased world commerce.

Rick's granddad had flown as one of the first enforcer squads after the I-LoC passed, targeting any unpiloted aircraft. That's back when pilots really flew; still amazing that Granddad had survived the Drone Wars. Finally gone were the days when a competitor would slam an untraceable drone into the engine of a cargo transport ship to up the value of their own goods. Murder by untraceable drone had moved from nation against nation to neighbor against neighbor during the DD.

You slept with my wife? A personal drone moving at Mach 1 hammered into your car while it was driving you to work. *You broke up with me, you bitch?* Poof! *Passed me over for promotion?* Boom!

Everyone agreed that the DD had been bad and no one wanted to go back there. So, wars had shifted to more conventional forms of killing people and relative safety returned to the skies, at least outside of atmo. Inside atmo, Earth just kept getting weirder and weirder, which was why so many nations were heading up the grav well.

The French had been the first to jump when they'd bugged out twenty years ago. They'd flown out to the asteroid belt, taken over Ceres, and—once they'd hollowed it out—crawled inside and closed the door with barely a *Bonne chance, Salope.* You too, bitch.

"Okay, Jess," he grabbed a food pack and tossing back a painkiller before holding the mission chip up against the reader. "Let's see what fun we're up to today."

* * *

Seal and secure.

Mission plan loaded.

Fuel = plan + 50%. Check.

Ammo = plan (0) + full charge COIL laser.

Air = sufficient 4 crew 6 months or full load 1 week + regen. Check.

All of Alpha Company. Check.

Shit! Earth. Going all of the way down to the surface? Ug-ly!

This and other titles are available at fine retailers everywhere.

Other works by M.L. Buchman

<u>The Night Stalkers</u>

MAIN FLIGHT
The Night Is Mine
I Own the Dawn
Wait Until Dark
Take Over at Midnight
Light Up the Night
Bring On the Dusk
By Break of Day

WHITE HOUSE HOLIDAY
Daniel's Christmas
Frank's Independence Day
Peter's Christmas
Zachary's Christmas
Roy's Independence Day

AND THE NAVY
Christmas at Steel Beach
Christmas at Peleliu Cove

5E
Target of the Heart
Target Lock on Love

<u>Firehawks</u>

MAIN FLIGHT
Pure Heat
Full Blaze
Hot Point
Flash of Fire

SMOKEJUMPERS
Wildfire at Dawn
Wildfire at Larch Creek
Wildfire on the Skagit

Delta Force
Target Engaged
Heart Strike

Angelo's Hearth
Where Dreams are Born
Where Dreams Reside
Maria's Christmas Table
Where Dreams Unfold
Where Dreams Are Written

Eagle Cove
Return to Eagle Cove
Recipe for Eagle Cove
Longing for Eagle Cove
Keepsake for Eagle Cove

Deities Anonymous
Cookbook from Hell: Reheated
Saviors 101

Dead Chef Thrillers
Swap Out!
One Chef!
Two Chef!

SF/F Titles
Nara
Monk's Maze

The Elsie and Me Chronicles (and Jen too)

Newsletter signup at:
www.mlbuchman.com